THAT SUMMER AT THE METTAWAS

THAT SUMMER

at the Mettawas

by
Rosalind Knight

CRANBERRY TREE PRESS
WINDSOR, ONTARIO, CANADA

Author can be contacted at: rosalind_knight@hotmail.com.

First printing, January 2014.
Printed in Canada

Library and Archives Canada Cataloguing in Publication Data

Knight, Rosalind, author
            That summer at the Mettawas / Rosalind Knight.

ISBN 978-1-894668-59-0 (pbk.)

            I. Title.

PS8621.N553T43 2014   C813'.6   C2013-908583-1

For Andrew, Allison, Lauren
and their Great-Great Aunt Betsy.

A blessing bring, and be thou blest,
Rest a whyle, and then God speed.
Fair hap be thine on land and foam,
And joy attend each coming home.

PROLOGUE

≈

June 1900 – Kingsville

*B*ETSY STEPPED UP into the carriage while the driver picked up the reins, waiting for the several passengers to be seated on the woollen blanket covering the bench. The team of greys snorted, anxious to trot down the tree-lined street to the Mettawas Hotel just a short distance from the train station. She could smell – almost taste – the tang in the air, a mixture of leather, damp wool, and something unfamiliar: an earthy – no, a fishy smell.

The young woman looked ahead toward the lake. Before her she could just make out the activity at the entranceway to a grand building three storeys high with many windows and balconies. Her heart pounded.

"I do hope that some of the girls I met last year shall return for summer work," said Kitty, the new acquaintance she had just made at the train station. "We all had such a wonderful time," she added.

Once they had arrived at their destination and alighted from the omnibus, Betsy could only look up and around with awe and trepidation. The tourist pamphlets were exactly right: the resort was, indeed, a kind of paradise on the lake away from the business of the city. Before her a magnificent building, to her right another smaller one, and all around, colourful gardens and thick groves of trees.

A magnificent setting, Betsy thought, and she had yet to even fully appreciate the lake itself and its beautiful harbour.

Despite the distracting beauty of these new surroundings, Betsy's mind turned momentarily to her betrothed, soon to arrive in Canada. She was looking forward to the day he would travel here from England. For now, though, Betsy quickly fell into step with the other girls, all anxiously awaiting what adventures the summer would bring.

CHAPTER 1

≈

April 17, 2000 – Kingsville

I WAKE UP IN the early morning hours to the wailing of sirens and clanging of fire trucks. Graeme and I think the sounds originate by the lake. Though we live a few miles away outside the town of Kingsville, I can smell the acrid smoke when I open the bedroom window just a crack. I quickly close it, but not before I stare to the south in the direction of Lake Erie. The pre-dawn sky is both dark and light – an eerie combination. Three miles away, thick grey smoke is at that very moment belching upwards as white-hot flames curl away from the abandoned building's roof. What we do not yet know, but what will reveal itself as the day plays out, is that the old, derelict Lakeshore Terrace Hotel will lie ravaged, a mere smouldering rubble, victim of years of neglect and probable arson.

The event loosens tongues. In the town's grocery store,

3

barber shop, and that quintessential nerve centre, the coffee shop, patrons speculate about what really has occurred. Suddenly everyone is an expert. *"Accident about to happen,"* some say. *"The building has been abandoned for years. What did anyone expect?"*

Graeme and I read *The Windsor Star* at our breakfast bar. More like skim the pages while we eat cereal and down coffee, I think, since we'll head out to work within the hour. Both Graeme and I are high school teachers. He drives to the neighbouring town of Essex, while my destination is only five minutes away. I have found the story the next day on the third page – 'the local scene' – and we both read the article with interest, having lived all our married life in the town of Kingsville. Both of us can remember the Lakeshore in its heyday as a popular tourist destination, first as a hotel and then primarily for its popular smorgasbords in the 60s and 70s.

"Before we were married we used to go to that little bar downstairs at the Lakeshore. What was its name?" I ask my husband.

Graeme pours another cup of coffee and reads the page over my shoulder. "You mean the Choo Choo Stop? Yeah – we used to have some fun there." He chuckles as he recalls those hot summer nights, a cold drink or two, a few laughs at a small table with friends, a sexy dance on the small wooden dance floor right in front of the live band belting out a tune like "Rocky Mountain Way."

"What a shame. It says here that the building sat empty for seven years." I rarely drive down there by the park, but when I did go past there recently, I was shocked to see what that property had become. "Some of the windows had been broken and boarded up, there was graffiti on the sign outside, and generally it was a real mess," I say.

I stand up and take my dishes to the sink. "When I was a little girl, on the odd Saturday when we were at our cottage over on Cedar Beach, my family used to go to the Lakeshore for a special dinner."

"Yeah," continues Graeme, "I know even when I was in high school, there used to be busloads of tourists – usually Americans – coming out to the lake from Windsor." We quickly peruse the other pages of the paper in silence.

Busy day coming up. I consider what I have to do after school and then my brain freezes on my mother's situation. After today's staff meeting I plan to visit Mama in the long-term care facility in town. She's now ninety years old. Dementia has taken its toll in the last few years, at first encroaching on her ability to remember the names of friends, and then the details of everyday life, until living alone became dangerous to her well-being. Eventually, even her language skills diminished.

Still, as recent as six years ago, my mother was living alone in her own house in Windsor. She had managed for a few years on her own after my father died, but it soon became apparent that it was not safe for her to remain there by herself. She would never have agreed to leave the place where she had lived all her married life with Daddy, so my sisters and I had to trick her into moving to the retirement home.

"Try it for a month," we encouraged her. "It will be temporary," we said, "only for as long as we're away on vacation and unable to help you." But we really knew otherwise, even when we returned. One month turned into several, until after a year and a half, Mama had to be transferred to the nearby nursing home.

Putting this aside for now, I continue to get ready for work.

I glance at my watch as I walk through the heavy automated doors of the Royal Court long-term care facility. It had been a longer staff meeting than usual. Now to go through the routine. Sign in. Use hand sanitizer. Walk down the corridor to my mother's 'neighbourhood', euphemism for her wing in the building. Round the nurses' station I go, and see the regulars in their wheelchairs, parked beside each other against the wall, like old roadsters taken off the busy highway. I nod at one or two who smile at me, wave at others, try to call them by their names when I can. A few just stare blankly at me, perhaps trying to place who I am and what I'm doing there; others doze, slumped over or sideways in their wheelchairs. Once again it occurs to me that it takes a special person to work here among human beings whose advanced years have transformed them into people entirely different from the vital mothers, fathers, wives, and husbands they used to be.

"Hi, Mama!" I smile as I approach her sitting in her wheelchair. At first I notice the puzzled look on her face, then a flash of something like recognition registers and she smiles as I plant a kiss on her cheek. I rub between her shoulders with one hand. I hope she knows me today, though I can't be sure. I could be a daughter or a sister in her world where time weaves together and becomes knotted and meaningless to her.

"Have you seen Mother today?" she asks me – so I have the answer to the recognition question. Her mother died forty years ago.

I've learned not to try to explain the real world to her. I shake my head and answer, "No, not today."

It makes me sad to think that she was once very athletic and socially vibrant, and now advanced age has crippled her so that she requires assistance for everything. I know that if Mama could see herself now, she would be most indignant about her situation. She struggles to follow the conversation, but more and more doesn't seem to care about taking part in any dialogue. I understand that her only real connection to the world is in the here and now. So, I'll often wear a bright floral blouse knowing that she will nod with approval at my choice, or I'll deliberately wear a sparkling brooch or necklace to draw her attention, and that always works. Her eyes at first light up, but then she might look down at her own unadorned hands, bent and twisted with arthritis and frown as if she knows she has lost something else of value.

As usual, we walk through the neighbourhoods, me pushing the chair. She mentions at every turn the 'long hall', and I think, yes, it certainly is.

A linen cart with the word 'Soiled' on the hamper affixed to it blocks our way, and I slip to one side of the corridor. For the first time I glance at this particular wall and notice enlarged, grainy, black and white framed photographs: the harbour with its long wooden dock and steamships in the water; the old railway station; some pictures from various perspectives of a beautiful, elegant building with balconies and many windows.

"Here – let me move this out of your way," says a personal support worker, which breaks my concentration. She moves the cart to the other side of the hall. I push the chair along and we continue our little journey down and around the hallways. Finally we come full circle, back to her room. I kiss her cheek once again and say I'll see her soon, and she nods, closes her eyes, and falls asleep.

The drive home brings me to consider what my sisters and I call 'our situation', which basically is the need to finally part with the family cottage. Jean, Elaine, and I have unloaded the house in Windsor, but our family's cottage is a long way from being put up for sale. It's full of furniture, dishes, even clothes, and the stuff has accumulated over decades. One thing about Mama even when she had her wits about her was that she could never part with her things, would never entertain the notion that it might be time to start to divest herself of her belongings. Now when I consider it, I realize her encroaching dementia might have been half the culprit, robbing her of the ability to take stock of her life and consider that it might be time to declutter and downsize.

"But it's way beyond time," I mutter. Since I live in the

area and my sisters don't, I have the power of attorney over her property and health.

Now it's up to the three of us to finally tackle the cottage and get it ready for listing. Today's description in the newspaper of the abandoned building's demise reminds me of the urgency of ridding ourselves of the old place. My thoughts turn to what I need to do first. In a couple of weeks Graeme and I will turn on the water at the cottage and start the process of delving into its contents until my sisters can arrive to help. It won't be easy. Or much fun.

CHAPTER 2

≈

May, 2000 – Cedar Beach

*H*E HAD PART of a finger missing on one hand. I'm reading information given on the passports of my great Uncle Norman and my great Aunt Betsy. What a weird, old paper relic, I think, as I peruse the single passport with both their pictures. They have been deceased now for decades. The document, along with the several papers and pictures Graeme and I discover in one of several closets of the family's cottage, has been stored inside an antique tin biscuit box.

"I didn't know Aunt Betsy was a year older than Uncle Norman. Isn't it funny how they used to describe people in official documents? They could never get away with this today." I continue to handle the yellowed paper to see their pictures and read the statements that the government of the time had deemed relevant for people immigrating to Canada. "There's a place here where the officer is supposed to describe the height of their brows and the length of their noses, as well as comment on other distinguishing features, such as the fact my great uncle had lost the tip of his finger, probably something to do with his occupation. It says here Uncle Norman was a 'meat cutter'."

"I believe it," says Graeme. "Look at all this stuff." He opens a heavy canvas kit and lays out its contents on the floor. Cleavers and odd looking knives of various sizes, now rusted, a few blades nicked or broken. I watch him continue to pull out forgotten items hidden in the closet in the tiny back bedroom. There are so many things packed in there. Out comes a bedroll of feather ticking, a few vintage lithographs with cracked glass, and images foxed from decades of being shut away in a hot, humid place. Added to the emerging pile are two enamelled pots, a kerosene lamp, and a mildewed canvas duffel bag, the contents of which I'll sort through later.

Incredible that for all the summers I spent as a kid in this room the closet was always locked or inaccessible to me. In fact, my mother had moved my furniture – limited as it was – so that something always blocked the door of this storage area. For the longest time I didn't even know it was there. From the outside I scrutinize the closet's open door which blends into the tongue-and-groove wooden walls and ceiling. In front of the closet had always been my small iron cot or wooden dresser, depending on how we had set up the bedroom after the family's traditional spring cleaning. I didn't need the storage space; I used to hang my own clothes from a rope suspended in a small recessed corner nook. I wonder whether my parents had even known what was kept here, and decide that my mother in particular just did not want to have to deal with throwing anything out. *Trying to decide what to discard and what to keep in readying the place for sale will not be an easy job,* I think.

Today Graeme and I are targeting this small back bedroom only. Each of the other three bedrooms have similar closets, all stuffed with who-knows-what that Aunt Betsy and Uncle Norman had hidden away even before our family came on the scene to spend fifty summers here.

Compared to my two sisters, I am the most emotionally attached to the cottage. All my best memories of growing up derive from my adventures here. Digging in the sand under the hot summer sun. Diving through the crested waves at the sandbar with my sisters, my mother lounging and bobbing on an inner tube beside us. Walking down the road just after dawn and again before dusk with Daddy and Zippy. Riding my bicycle to meet someone. First love. First heartache.

This bedroom in particular had been my summer sanctuary from the time I was just a baby until I left home to marry. My parents had inherited this house on Cedar Beach in 1953, shortly after my dad's uncle, Norman Parker, had passed away. At the time of his death, Daddy's Aunt Betsy would have been in her mid-seventies, unable to live here alone.

I think now of Aunt Betsy and her husband who died the year I was born. I know so little of their life together.

How difficult it must have been for her to leave the only real home she had known with my uncle, and how generous of her to give our family the gift of this place. Funny how I never really thought of that before.

After Uncle Norman's death, Aunt Betsy had moved to Leaver's Rest Home on Victoria Avenue in Windsor where she could be close to her sister, Emily, who lived a few miles away on the east side of the city in an area still proudly called Walkerville by its citizens, even after amalgamation with Windsor. With no children of their own to inherit their place on the lake, the Parkers had allowed for their year-round home to become our family's summer retreat. Every June my mother and father, two sisters, our dog, and I would leave the heat of the city immediately after school was out for the summer and enjoy two glorious months at Cedar Beach on Lake Erie. Since my father had been an elementary school principal, he had been free to spend the summer months with us, unencumbered by the bustle of the city.

Start to focus on the task at hand, I think. *Enough memories.* The heat is rising upstairs, rendering the air stuffy and uncomfortable. I peer at Graeme, deep inside the closet. He's being a real trooper with this dirty job while I just daydream.

"Hey, Graeme — I'm glad you're wearing that gauze mask you brought with you today," I say. "There must be all kinds of mould and dust around. Guess I'm not much use here since only one of us can fit in there at a time, so why don't I start to haul stuff downstairs and pile things in the middle of the living room? It should be cooler down there anyway." Most of the junk seems to us mere curiosity pieces. Some of the items that Graeme pulls out and piles in the middle of the room are hard to identify, relics from another era.

"Hey – can you hear me in there?"

In response, Graeme emerges from the stifling confines of the hole in the wall and pulls off the white gauze mask. His sweat-lined face is murky with grime. He draws a forearm across his brow. At his feet, the spoils of his victory, with the pile reaching into the hallway.

"What's that? Oh, yeah. I actually need a change of scenery. I'll help you carry everything downstairs and we'll just call it a day."

"Sounds like a plan. That way we can have everything out in the open and when Jean and Elaine arrive in two weeks, we'll be better able to decide what we keep and what gets tossed."

My sisters and their husbands, one couple from Montreal, the other from Toronto, will be coming to stay with us for a few days. They say that they respect my judgment enough for me to discard anything that I deem to be junk. My plan is to get the most obvious things ready for garbage collection before my sisters even arrive. The long weekend – Victoria Day – is coming soon, the ideal time for the six of us to make the hard decisions of who will take what in terms of the antiques that are here. If the past exercise of selling the house in Windsor is a measure of what we can expect in the future, I anticipate no sibling problems.

Still, there are so many memories. When I look outside this window I can visualize how it used to be. "Let me have a minute, Graeme. I'll see you downstairs."

I close my eyes, take a deep breath, open them again and am transported back in time. I part the flimsy curtains covering the windows, look out and see the back road as it used to be with the marshy field beyond. I smile at the memory of a friend coming over to play, crossing the shared lawns (no fences between cottages then!), walking up the cement path leading to the cottage, knocking on the back door, asking for me in a singsong voice, making my name sound as if it has three long syllables. *"Beth-ee-ee!"* We take turns pushing each other in wagons. Ride bicycles. Haul buckets of sand from the beach to make cakes for our 'bakery'. Build a raft. I imagine our family's sleek black 1959 Pontiac parked at the end of the driveway.

It's again 1963 with a young Dobson family tumbling out of the vehicle, primed to get the cottage ready for a two-month summer vacation at the beach. Zippy, a black-and-white spaniel mix, leads the way.

CHAPTER 3

≈

Victoria Day weekend – Cedar Beach, 1963

"NO ONE GO inside empty-handed. Bethie, you take in Mama's brownies so I know they'll be well taken care of," James Dobson said, winking at his youngest daughter while the two older girls, Jean, eighteen, and Elaine, sixteen, rolled their eyes, their arms laden with heavy boxes filled with canned goods and food for stocking the kitchen. James's silver brush cut and youthful grin belied his sixty-three years of age. He had married late in life; his wife, Mary, was thirteen years his junior. Beth had been their 'miracle' child, arriving while Mary was forty. Maybe it was this young family that fostered his boyish spirit, despite the fact he was two years away from retirement.

The water in the cottage had been turned on last Saturday. Now the big weekend task was to clean the whole place and enjoy the Victoria Day holiday, and then have the cottage primed and ready for when school was out for the summer holidays. As happened every first week of the summer, they would be bringing out James's Aunt Betsy from the nursing home to enjoy what used to be hers until her husband died a decade ago. Ten-year-old Beth asked the question anyway: "Is Aunt Betsy coming out with us when school gets out?"

"Yup. You know the drill. We'll come out first for a few days to be sure that everything here is all set, and then your mother and I will drive back to Windsor to pick her up. So today everyone has to pitch in to help. We have to put our best foot forward, you know." James turned to his other two girls who were already starting to lug boxes from the car. "Okay, everyone, let's get to it."

Beth tried to lift a box from the trunk of the car, but it was too heavy.

"Beth, take this in to your mother." James handed Beth a pillowcase filled with clean towels. "I've got the perfect job for you, young lady. Stand there at the door and get ready to open it every time one of us approaches with our arms full." He turned to the other two girls. "I'd like you to start with the kitchen, then all three of you will be responsible for cleaning your own bedrooms. Once we have everything in the house, I'll tackle Auntie's room."

The day promised to be sunny but damp, typical Essex County spring weather at the lake. They could hear the thrilling trill of the red-winged blackbirds that perched on milkweed pods and bulrushes across the road, lining the wet marshlands. Beth was anxious to get this early summer cleaning over and done with. Inside, Jean and Elaine would soon be washing all the dishes that had not been used during the winter when the place had been closed up tight. Mary would supervise Beth's efforts in her own bedroom.

But there was also much to do outside – shells to collect and stones to skip across the expanse of calm grey lake. Beth could hardly wait for the best job of all, which was to keep Zippy from being underfoot. Eventually she and the dog would keep counsel the better part of the day by sitting together at the end of the dock, surveying sky and lake. But for now, there was dusting and lemon-oiling of all wood surfaces, swishing out of curtains, sweeping of linoleum floors.

As the youngest, Beth seemed to be given preferential treatment by their parents, at least according to her older sisters. Mary Dobson would inevitably take pity on her little girl – who kept sighing audibly at the jobs at hand – eventually relieving her of many of the tasks, including the making of her own bed. Beth was always wary of the heavy eiderdown which her mother would place folded at the end of her bed on top of the chenille bedspread. After all, who knew what creepy crawlers lurked there in the folds of the fabric. When a chilly lakeside morning arrived, however, she would be grateful for the eiderdown's warmth.

Once outside and unfettered by indoor drudgery, Beth turned up her face to enjoy the warm sun. With a short whistle to Zippy, the two approached one of her favourite places – the wooden dock reaching out into the water at the side of their property – where they sat together, Beth curling her arm around Zippy's neck, anticipating the summer fun. She admired the sandy beach they had; the water level seemed low. She could feel the heat from the dock's wooden planks beneath her legs, feel her eyes dazzled by the rays of sun glinting off the water's surface.

She turned to squint at the cottage, now behind her. The two-storey 'summer house' as her mother called it, was bigger than the two smaller cottages beside it. Their shape and design looked similar, though, with cement block exteriors textured to resemble cut-stone, a popular architectural style of the early twentieth century. The front porches were enclosed with large windows on all three sides. Beth's great Uncle Norman, Betsy's husband, had built all three places a long time ago, though she had never considered when that time was. At ten years of age, all she knew and cared about was that when her father's uncle had died, her family had inherited the bigger house where Norman had lived with Betsy, having sold the neighbouring smaller two cottages years before when he was still a young man. So Beth had spent every summer of her life at Cedar Beach.

Aunt Betsy and Uncle Norman never had any children of their own; they had always considered James and his brother, Eddie, the sons they never had. When James had children of his own, his three daughters were as close as Betsy and Norman would ever get to having a complete family. Their other nephew, Eddie, had married but also had no children. So the Dobsons inherited the place. Now, for one week at the beginning of summer vacation and for one week toward its end, the Dobsons would invite Aunt Betsy to visit and stay with them. Even Beth's ten-year-old brain could recognize the old lady's importance in the grand scheme of things. Her two weeks at the cottage with them was a small price to pay (as Beth's parents would constantly remind their children) for a whole summer of fun.

Beth decided she could put up with ancient Aunt Betsy and her false teeth floating in a glass half-filled with water. She was a curiosity, an elderly woman with a deaf ear, a soft whistle when she played euchre, a failing memory, and yet, if only Beth would really listen, a surprising story to tell.

CHAPTER 4

≈

May, 2000 — Cedar Beach

*I*T'S NO EASY matter to turn off emotion triggered by memory, especially since working here at the cottage is like entering a time machine. Orange flowered wallpaper that Mama had put up in the kitchen is peeling and discoloured in places from mildew. At least at the time of the cottage renovation in the 60s, those walls matched the multi-coloured shag rug on the living room floor, though I wonder what nasty things might have hunkered down in its fibres over four decades. In the corner is the faded blue upholstered chair with wooden arms, now darkened from years of wear. I imagine my father sitting there, book in hand, legs crossed, one arm dangling down to scratch Zippy's head. I can even hear my dad express aloud the wonderful pleasure of touching a dog's cold nose.

I walk through the living room into the enclosed porch

and think once again how all the windows around the perimeter allow in the light of day. This room can always boost my mood, even now. I look to one side and can see with my mind's eye my sisters playing *Clue* with their friends at an old pedestal table painted an odd colour that my father called 'Cuban Cocoa', a colour he claimed he had created by blending leftover paint. Here are pieces of original wicker furniture that had belonged to my Aunt Betsy. I raise my eyes above the door where my mother years ago had put up a sign she had bought at a flea market: *"You are a stranger here but once"* it announces to all who enter. I take down the sign, think for only a minute whether I should keep it for sentimental reasons, and then toss it on top of the pile of stuff.

Both Graeme and I survey the growing mound of artefacts. For several days now we have been working steadily at cleaning out the walk-in storage closets in all four bedrooms upstairs, and the mound is growing into a small mountain. This weekend, Jean and Elaine will arrive with their husbands. I anticipate discussions about what to keep, what to discard.

The more obvious junk we take to the road. By putting out things today, we know that the people who enjoy trawling before early morning trash pickup will be out in full force. Some pieces are difficult to part with, but we hope that someone else's discerning eye can spot potential treasure. We add to the pile.

"Look at this nice brass pole lamp--it would be great if someone knew how to rewire it safely," Graeme says, pausing to take a deep breath after hauling piece after piece to the road. "Look at these! I'd better re-wrap these old rusty cleavers and knives more securely in their canvas kit. They look dangerous. I can't believe they could be of any use to anyone now, except maybe as a curiosity." Graeme wraps part of a frayed cord around the material holding the knives, and then tucks the whole kit under some old, musty pillows.

"I can't believe those two slipper chairs from upstairs have been plucked already from the side of the road," I say. "The lady who stopped to haul them into the back of her pickup this morning told me she was delighted with them, even though they're threadbare and smelly. She said she would strip them down to their frames and then rebuild them good as new. She thought the frames would be made of solid wood.... I hope she'll enjoy them after all the work it will take to make them presentable. I'm actually kind of embarrassed by the way they look now."

I take a tissue from my jean pocket, blow my nose, and narrow my eyes, which are watering from sweat and dust. "Wow, I'm beat! Let's call it a day!"

With a few more decisions to make before leaving, we walk up the path leading to the back of the cottage, regard the few small furniture pieces that lie on the grass under the kitchen window. Outside in the light of day we can clearly see what's wrong with them. One chair has a broken cane seat; a once beautiful walnut nightstand is warped from dampness and neglect. The glass, cut to fit the top surface perfectly, has done the wood no favours over the years. Humid conditions have caused the air-deprived tabletop to crack and chip. I know that each piece has its own story, but I'm in no mood for that right now.

Graeme puts into words what I'm feeling. "What can you expect when no one has lived here for a few years? Here's a good case for divesting ourselves of things while we can. Makes me want to sit Sarah down and say, okay, what stuff of ours do you want to have?"

I smirk at him, all the time knowing that essentially what he's saying is right.

"Your mother refused to part with things, especially after your father's death. Now the humidity and dampness and plain neglect of the place have taken their toll."

I guess he's tired, I think. *He sure isn't mincing words.*

I'm tired as well and start to tune out his rant. I steady my gaze on an unusual wooden chair with a high back that he has tossed on the ground. I consider it, and then can feel myself grin as I remember the old piece. The oak frame is split and falling apart, but what catches my attention is the large hole in the wood where the seat should be.

"You know what, Graeme? Here's Aunt Betsy's old commode. I haven't seen it in ages. With a little wood glue, we could make this into a great planter – a real conversation starter!"

"Are you kidding me?" is the reply. He takes another cleansing breath, gearing up for my pitch.

"Look here," I say, and grab one of the four chamber pots strewn on the ground. I hold it in my hand, but feel my nose wrinkle when I see the stain of yellow inside it.

"The pot goes on the floor with the chair's hole positioned above it, and voilà! A portable toilet! I guess they wouldn't have had indoor plumbing when Uncle Norman first built this place. Or maybe at night they might not have wanted to go outside to the outhouse. I remember Daddy saying that he used to come here as a little boy with his brother, Eddie, to visit his aunt and uncle during the summer, and I know from stories he told us that they hadn't yet built the small extension off the kitchen where the toilet and sink are now. He had to put one of these under his bed. Kind of cool, eh?"

Another memory insinuates itself into my brain, like a slide dropping into view, an image of the tiny bathroom just off the kitchen, and then one of Aunt Betsy's downstairs bedroom and the commode sitting in the corner. Aunt Betsy would insist that the commode be in her room, despite our indoor plumbing. A sudden visual makes me smile: the image of the old woman dumping into the toilet the contents of the chamber pot in the morning. The thought of her bare bottom sitting on the chair, poised over the pot, still makes me chuckle. As a young girl I remember feeling both awe and horror trying to come to terms with the rituals of an ancient relative.

"Oh come on, Graeme!" The look of disbelief on his face makes me laugh. "If nothing else, this will make a fabulous stand for a flower pot at the back door. Don't worry — we don't have to take the pot," I tease, and give Graeme a squeeze on the elbow, a peck on the cheek. I know I have already won the argument.

With a few pieces of furniture and a pile of items inside the house awaiting the final verdict from my sisters this weekend, and with another pile at the road to be picked over by strangers, we finally pull behind us the heavy wooden door and lock the house. The late afternoon's spring lake air feels cooling to our flushed faces. We climb into our car to return home only four miles away on the Jack Miner Road, tired but pleased so much has been accomplished today.

Graeme drives as I allow my eyes to close. I have put in the trunk a couple of pictures to see if their frames can be salvaged, and also what is left of the old wooden commode. I cannot shake the memory of Aunt Betsy and some of the odd things she used to say to me when I was a little girl. Strange how her idiosyncrasies and peculiar comments still transfix me. I just need to make sense of them.

CHAPTER 5

≈

May 24th weekend, 2000 – Kingsville

M Y HUSBAND'S JOHN Deere hat, green to match his lawn mower, is pulled down low on his forehead, which always makes Sarah and me laugh since he never wears a hat.

"Such a funny ritual of his," Sarah has said to me before.

And it really is some kind of odd routine. The hat always goes on his head before he cuts the lawn. Right now he is riding his revered machine back and forth, cutting a swath through the half acre of grass. Lots of things for me to do, too, I think, before Jean and Rick, Elaine and Mike arrive later on. At least the two guest rooms are clean. Better tackle the rest of the to-do list. I feel glad that Sarah will be home from Western for the long holiday weekend.

Instead of working, though, I pause to admire the small goldfinches at the bird feeder outside the kitchen window.

I observe a large blue jay descend, causing the feeder to rock back and forth, the smaller birds to skitter in all directions, seeds to fall on the ground below. Another beautiful spring morning, a promising start to the day.

Thoughts of chores and guests' arrival times intrude on my tranquil moment at the window. We'll have a full house for a few days, I think, and open up the freezer. I pull out the package of steaks and place it on the counter to thaw. It will be good to see Sarah, but she'll spend much of the holiday weekend with her friends. I know that I'll enjoy time with Jean and Elaine and their husbands. Then I think of Mama and how pleased she would have been to see us all together again, though if her faculties were intact, she sure would not appreciate how we are going to pick over the possessions she once considered so valuable.

I think a lot lately about items of value and things that hold none at all, except for sentimental reasons. So many household items have stories attached to them, especially those antiques. What are their stories? Who used to enjoy eating from those dishes or drinking from those teacups? I look at the crystal vase with flowers I bought specifically for tonight's barbecue, and wonder if someday when Graeme and I have gone Sarah will just discard or give away the things she has no use for, or doesn't see any value in, real or sentimental. I can almost see that happening. Sarah's university apartment is sparsely furnished, just the way she likes it. She's immersed in her own life these days, gets home when she can, though it seems she prefers now to be in London with her friends.

And then I have to consider all those photographs and documents that I've stored in bins and put down in the basement. "I'll get to them someday," I mutter to myself, and think instead of the magnitude of the task at hand this weekend. The garage door closes; Graeme enters the foyer.

"What time are we expecting everyone?" he asks, taking off his shoes on the mat.

"Well, I know Jean is already halfway here because they stayed in Toronto last night, and Elaine said they would try to arrive just after lunch. Fortunately, they both drive vans. They'll need them! Sarah should be here any time now."

From the kitchen cupboard I take out the dishes for dinner, and set them on the table.

"I expect we'll be able to hit the cottage for a couple of hours later this afternoon. The big thing is to decide if they want any of the furniture pieces that they'll have to cart home. I'd like to have everything that we've piled in the middle of the living room floor either discarded, taken by one of us, or packed in boxes for the Legion's summer rummage sale," I say. *At least that's the plan.*

The plan seems sensible enough. By mid-afternoon after my sisters and their husbands have arrived, we all find ourselves foraging through the cottage. I'm grateful that we have the kind of relationship where we can be honest and direct without hurting each other's feelings.

"I love what you've done with the place," Jean jokes as she looks with mock horror at the various mounds of stuff on the floor. "Shouldn't take too long to go through this junk." She picks up and then quickly discards an old canvas bag. All of us become intent on the project, though it soon becomes clear that unlike my sisters who have little interest in some of the items, I need to discuss each one before tossing or keeping it.

Inside a box is a stack of Superman comics. "Remember how I used to bring all kinds of things into the cottage from the beach, and you two would get rather annoyed? I used to bring all shapes and sizes of small stones into my room, and then paint them the various colours of Kryptonite when I was playing 'Superman', remember?"

This draws blank stares.

"Really? You don't remember that?" I continue. "You would complain that my paint was making the upstairs smell. I don't think Mama and Daddy really cared because it kept me occupied. Well, at least it was alright until Mama discovered I had been using her guest towels as capes." I smile as I remember my interest in all things Superman when I was about ten years old. "And don't you remember how I would bring those Junebugs into the kitchen and try to train them?"

After some sisterly teasing, Jean and Elaine shift their attention away from me to closely examine the walnut desk, also part china cabinet, now emptied of its contents.

"You know, Beth, I seem to remember this place differently from you. I don't recall being here so much. Some of us had to work in the summer, you know," says Jean with an exaggerated look of disapproval at me. "First it was part-time at Layman's shoe store, but I remember making some good money for going away to university when I was hired to wash dishes on Sundays at the Lakeshore. I was actually kind of saddened that it burnt down last month."

"Yeah, Jean's right," Elaine adds. "Not everyone under this roof had the luxury of play, you know," she says, contributing gently to the teasing at my expense. She pauses in her examination of the desk, retrieving some of her own memories.

"If you were to ask me, I'd say that my fondest memories revolve around being a counsellor at the Kiwanis Sunshine Camp down the road. Let's see. I think I worked there for a month for several summers after I turned sixteen. I have to admit, though, that I have some really great memories of going to Cedar Island in the evenings to meet my friends at that little store that had a jukebox. I forget its name…." At this last reflection, Elaine's voice trails off. We can all recall how her antics with her teenaged friends often were the source of our parents' frustration and worry.

Now all three of us examine the contents of this unique piece of furniture.

"This is really neat," Jean offers. "Even with some of the exterior veneer stripped away, I think this is a real find. If you two aren't interested in it, we'll take it!"

"Okay by me," Elaine says, and I have to agree. Some of these things have not been used in so long that a really offensive, musty smell emanates from them.

Suddenly, as we take out each drawer, we notice an envelope taped to the underside of one.

"Yeah! Maybe this is the long-lost treasure we've been hoping to find!" Elaine quips.

Jean gently lifts the envelope, which tears a little from the movement of the drawer, but it lifts easily as the yellowed tape which secured it to the wood has lost its stickiness. Inside the envelope there are several newspaper clippings, now yellowed. There are a few from *The Kingsville Reporter* about the destruction of a place called the Mettawas Resort in 1903; one about the construction of a smaller Mettawas Inn in 1914; another which focuses on the same inn with a name change to the Lakeshore Terrace Hotel which, at the time of the clippings in 1953, had just been sold. There's a clipping or two from *The Amherstburg Echo* as well.

"Darn!" Jean and Elaine both say at the same time.

"No fortune found here!" Elaine adds.

"I'll take those. Don't throw them away," I say, and snatch them before my sisters can toss them. I want to read them later when things settle down. Before putting the articles back into the envelope, I look at the discoloured paper, at the picture of the original place called 'Mettawas', and am stunned by how beautiful it must have been, judging from the image, though its details are indistinct.

Where did this magnificent place exist? What happened to it? I can't help but wonder why the clipping is taped to the drawer. Something sticks in my memory, but I just can't frame in my mind what it is. Then it comes to me.

Aunt Betsy used to work at a place down by the lake when she had just come over from England. But once Aunt Betsy died in — *let's see — was it in the mid-60s?* — our parents rarely talked about her, so I knew little more than

32

that. A few questions directed at my sisters make me realize that they know even less about her than I do.

"I was young, so of course I wouldn't be working," I remind them. I can remember Aunt Betsy's visits, and actually even enjoyed those rare times when the old woman seemed to befriend me, maybe almost confide in me, now that I really think about it. I also remember that Aunt Betsy suddenly fell ill during her last visit with us in late August, and she never did recover enough to return to the cottage and the town that she must have loved so much. In fact, if memory serves me correctly, she died the following winter.

It's almost as if my brain has been working on a puzzle which it finally has solved because all of a sudden I recall where I have seen these images before – the framed pictures of the Mettawas Hotel and Casino on the wall at the nursing home. *I'll have to pay closer attention to them when I go next time,* I think to myself.

The hours wear on and we are left to our own thoughts as we continue to choose items and discard others. At least through it all we're able to maintain a sense of humour, which makes the task less onerous. Soon we pack the three vehicles with the spoils of the Dobson cottage, and anticipate sitting on our deck, each drinking a well-deserved cold one, and firing up the grill, laughing and teasing each other about our varied memories of those wonderful summers at the lake. I smile when I anticipate how Sarah rolls her eyes at my stories, though I know she enjoys them, too.

Inside our own car trunk rests several items, including

one old lithograph I remember seeing in Aunt Betsy's bedroom. It's now somewhat foxed beneath glass that, instead of serving as protection, unfortunately has allowed the humidity to stain its edges over time. It's called "The Wee Hostess" and shows a lovely smiling lady in formal dress, reaching out toward a small child who is bringing her a steaming cup of tea. On the back in faded, meticulous handwriting, the note, *"For Betsy and Norman on the occasion of their upcoming nuptials – most sincerely, Maxwell Wallace, Mettawas, 1900."*

I probably will toss the picture but salvage the oak frame. In a plastic bin brought from home I store curious photographs I've found, along with the newspaper clippings, the subjects of which will make fascinating reading when I make time for them.

CHAPTER 6

≈

June, 2000 – Kingsville

I GO THROUGH THE door leading to the utility room in the basement. Company is gone, Sarah is busy with her friends, and now, finally, I have time to open those plastic bins filled with odds and ends from the cottage clean-out. When you see the bins day after day, they start to blend in to the rest of the general mess. At least I've dealt with the bigger pieces of furniture.

"Sure will be nice when the place sells," I mutter half under my breath. For one thing, when it does we won't have to keep hauling the smaller mower into the trunk and tending to the lawn and weeds at the lake.

For some reason today I'm feeling guilty, probably because I can't help but project into the future. I wonder what Sarah will do with all this stuff some day if it's all still here. Guilt can be a strong motivator. I know my answer, and for some strange reason it actually makes me smile. She will just toss everything, so I shrug my shoulders, gear up to tackle the contents and sit down on the tile floor having opened the bin with the box of photographs and envelopes of news clippings.

First I examine a pile of faded black and white pictures of a variety of people and settings. In one snapshot I see Aunt Betsy as a young woman, sitting in front of the stone fireplace at the cottage. In another I see a young Uncle Norman in the kitchen, arm outstretched, no doubt with a treat in hand, bending toward a little dog standing up on two legs. There are several snapshots taken outside − various people sitting on a cement jetty leading out into the water, people I don't recognize. The sandy beach in the picture looks more expansive than the one I remember as a child. It certainly looks bigger than the current one, which today is just a huge pile of boulders brought in to protect the shoreline from further erosion.

I sift through the pictures. Now here's one I recognize, and it makes me smile. The photograph captures the experience that Daddy used to tell me about when he, his older brother, Eddie, and their parents Emily and Thomas − my grandparents − would visit Betsy and Norman's cottage. I look more closely at my father as a little boy, grinning at the camera, one eye squinting at the sun, and feel a pang of recognition as I see even at that early age the friendly smile of the man who would grow up to become my father. Sarah makes that same squinting grin when she poses for the camera while looking into the sun.

Here's a snapshot capturing two people on bicycles as they pedal toward the camera. He waves, laughs at the photographer; she contorts her face either in mock or real fear. Must be Uncle Norman and Aunt Betsy. I look more closely at the picture in hand: not Cedar Beach, it seems. A park, perhaps? There are many people milling about in the background amid picnic tables and swings. On the back, *"Pleasure Grove, 1900."*

I turn my attention next to a smiling black couple standing beside each other in a rather ornate looking hallway. The couple is grinning at whoever has taken the picture. On the back the inscription in steady handwriting reads, *"To both of you, from both of us, Love Hattie. Together always, thanks to 'Old Wash'."* Someone has carefully printed the date, *'1900'*, and *'Mettawas Hotel'*.

Another picture shows three laughing girls standing close together beside an old-fashioned fire engine, arms around each others' slim waists, and on the back, *"H., K., and B. at the Mettawas fire drill, June 1900."* I see a grand building in the background.

Before me yet another scene, one with an old black man sitting on the grass under a tree encircled by several young children – all white – seemingly held spellbound in his presence.

I can't seem to turn away from these images, particularly of the building or collection of buildings labelled 'Mettawas'. *How have I lived in Kingsville for so many years and not known of its existence?* It resembles a castle to me, a sprawling magnificent hotel on the hill overlooking the lake, set amid groves of mature trees. I examine several photos more closely. One building is separate from the other large one, a building with a conical turret labelled 'Casino', with ladies dressed in formal attire walking about outside on a grass covered hill, parasols in hand to shade them from the sun. With them are gentlemen in straw hats, frozen in conversation, as well as little boys in short pants and girls in dresses, caught in a moment of play.

A different perspective shows the same buildings at the top of a hill. Someone has printed 'Bridge of Sighs' and drawn an arrow to the part where one building joins another. The picture is taken from the lake and looking upward at the building, showing in the foreground the long wooden dock and ships coming into the sanctuary of the harbour, puffing their steam up into the sky.

This stunning resort really did exist here in our town at one time. Whatever happened to it?

I gaze closely at these pictures, wonder what life might have offered these people whose lives are documented in them. I have never really thought of my elderly ancestors as having young, vibrant lives. I realize with a pang of regret that I've not really thought of them at all.

CHAPTER 7

≈

July, 1963 — Cedar Beach, Kingsville

A S BEFITTING HER eighty-four years, Aunt Betsy always wore a tasteful, but usually dark-coloured dress, with a brooch at the neck or a high, lacy collar. She wore comfortable black shoes, the kind that had chunky heels but resembled boots with laces. She was slight of build but not frail, with a round, solemn face and grey hair long enough to be curled and pinned up at the nape.

Though ten-year-old Beth would not have known at the time, her Aunt Betsy was in the early stages of dementia which took her away from the family many times in the course of the day. It might manifest itself in a faraway look in her eye as she struggled to understand their words; it might take shape in her fixation on a past event. She would repeat stories about life before she married her husband, stories that rarely made sense.

The room where Aunt Betsy stayed during her summer visit with the Dobson family had actually been the former dining room when she had lived in the house from the time it was built in the early 1900s until her husband's death. Now converted to her bedroom, it was the only sleeping area downstairs. There were four bedrooms upstairs: one for parents, one for each of the three sisters, each with a heavy, patterned privacy drape over the entrance. At the base of the stairs was a canvas covered door that they would open just a crack in order to peer into this small room to see whether Aunt Betsy were up and about and dressed. Not a very sound arrangement since it meant that the Dobsons had to pass through Aunt Betsy's room in order to escape to the rest of the house. This caused considerable embarrassment on more than one occasion.

Once when Beth had quietly descended the stairs and pushed open the door an inch to gauge whether it was a good time to come downstairs or not, she had to backtrack quickly and return to the sanctuary of her room for a few more minutes. She had caught an unwelcome glimpse of Aunt Betsy's backside as she was pulling up her bloomers.

That wasn't the worst of it. Beth hated to admit it, but she was perversely drawn to the dentures floating in the half-filled glass of water that she might be able to glimpse if she came downstairs early enough. Taking stock of the room, Beth would see, in addition to the single iron bed, a small bedside table; a highboy with mirror; a portrait of an old-fashioned woman with a wide-brimmed hat; another framed picture of a woman in a parlour with small children, one handing her a cup of tea; and a strange wooden chair in the corner that she understood took the place of a toilet. Under this chair sat a white enamelled pot. Sometimes in the morning when Beth descended the stairs, a sour smell would assault her nostrils.

Today as she passed through the room, she noticed the teeth were not in the glass on the nightstand, the pot not under the chair. Aunt Betsy was at that minute returning to her room, pot in hand. Beth knew every day she would walk with it – carefully so as not to spill anything – and make her way across the living room, through the kitchen to the small bathroom. She would overturn the contents into the toilet, swirl clean water into it, and return it to its designated spot underneath the chair or 'commode', as she called it.

One thing about Aunt Betsy, she liked to do this daily ritual herself, despite the family's offers of assistance. She was a proud lady, independent of spirit, and Beth liked that about her. Even at the young age of ten, Beth valued being left alone and understood the need to do things her way. Just about all of her personal needs Aunt Betsy took care of herself, including the laundering of her intimate things. At least once during her visit she would stand at the old porcelain sink in the kitchen, fill it with water, and test it for what she considered to be suitable temperature for washing delicates.

"You must never have the water too hot as it fastens the dirt in," she would advise Beth, as if pronouncing some great life lesson.

After the scrubbing, rinsing, and wringing of her under-garments, she would take the items outside and allow Beth to help her peg them to the clothesline, suspended across the patch of lawn between their cottage and their neighbour's. Mary had captured this activity one day when she had round-ed the cottage with camera in hand and snapped a picture as Beth was handing a wooden clothes peg to Aunt Betsy.

"Hey, you two!" she had said to them. "Smile!"

Aunt Betsy had taken the peg from Beth with great ceremony and bowed to her with exaggerated flourish, her face turned toward Mary's camera and her mouth just be-ginning to turn upwards in a smile.

On any given day in that one-week visit, you could see an array of bloomers, camisoles, and perhaps a tea tow-el hanging on the line reaching from the corner of their house to the walnut tree outside the neighbour's window.

"So much better to allow the fresh air at them – the ladies prefer it," Aunt Betsy had said, though Beth had no idea who these ladies might be.

On a typical hot July day, Beth and her friend Sandy could be seen walking down the road having treated themselves to chocolate-covered soft ice cream cones from the Frostee Treat, just over the bridge a mile from the Dobson cottage. They had stopped talking to each other, intent on lapping quickly the chocolate coating now spilling over the cones and onto their hands.

The girls walked over the Cedar Creek Bridge, gazing

shyly at the several Negroes fishing off the sides, their lines extending down into the creek below. These dark-skinned American men were there every day to catch catfish. They were always quiet and respectful, yet seemed mysterious, nevertheless, and the thought of eating a type of fish that had never been served at home or even eaten by anyone she knew seemed strange to Beth as well.

Beth had never personally befriended a coloured person, though there were a couple of families attending Prince Edward Elementary School which she attended in Windsor. She had limited opportunities to associate with such people; she had only seen them operating elevators at Hudson's in Detroit, handing out towels in that store's washroom, and now, fishing off the bridge.

Beth thought about yesterday when she had accompanied her mother and Aunt Betsy into town. She had been sifting through the new comic book she had bought for a dime at Burrows when they had driven over the Cedar Creek Bridge on the way home. When she had looked up, she had seen that Aunt Betsy had taken a clear interest in the fishermen. *What had her aunt meant when she had waved at one and smiled?* Beth recalled the slight intake of breath of her mother who, she knew, discouraged any communication with these men. But today as she and Sandy passed by, she noticed that not even one looked up at them.

Once over the bridge, the two friends ran squealing toward the lake, and washed the chocolate mess from their hands and faces in the cool water.

Later, on the walk home, Sandy acknowledged a conversation she had overheard between her parents. "My mom says that Elaine was caught smoking down at Cedar Island on Saturday. That true?"

"Yeah, I guess, but they never tell me anything. I heard them talking on the porch, though. My mother said she had better not learn that Elaine had been smoking, that it was a filthy habit, not proper for a young lady. Then Elaine explained that she had been inside the store, putting nickels in the jukebox, that some of her friends were dancing. She said she was just drinking her pop, but that several kids were smoking around her. I guess the smoke smell stuck to her sweater."

"Yeah, right!" Sandy said, shaking her head, laughing in disbelief.

"Well, I'm not sure Mama believed her either because Elaine couldn't walk down to the Island with her friends the next two nights. And she probably won't be able to go into town this weekend for any of the Dominion Day ceremonies."

Once home, Sandy returned to her family's cottage, stopping first to scratch Zippy behind the ears. Beth walked inside, looking first at her friend as she was retreating. "See you tomorrow!" she called.

Mary was at the kitchen sink arranging flowers, knowing Betsy always commented on her beautiful bouquets. She glanced up at Beth entering the kitchen, took one look at what appeared to be chocolate smears on her daughter's blouse, and said, "I hope you didn't spoil your appetite, young lady!" Beth grinned and shrugged her shoulders.

44

Mary sighed and continued with her news. "Once Jean returns from Layman's, we'll eat. She may be a little later today because she's closing up shop."

Beth picked a grape from the fruit bowl her mother had placed on the counter and said, "Where's Daddy?"

"Raking the beach. Burying that smelly old fish before Zippy finds it." Beth was already passing through to the living room when her mother added, "Before you go outside to see him, run upstairs and ask your sister to turn down her music. She bought a new record by some group that has a silly insect name – Beetles, or something like that. Oh – try not to bother Auntie. She's resting."

On the way through the house to the door leading to the lake, Beth noticed that Aunt Betsy was stirring from an afternoon nap in the rocking chair on the front porch. She had hoped to make it through the room without the old woman cornering her, but it was too late. Aunt Betsy had caught her tiptoeing past, and with an outstretched arm, invited her to stay and keep her company.

"And what, child, have you been doing this afternoon?"

Beth filled her in on some of her recent adventures with Sandy. Playing Superman. Riding bicycles. Collecting stones. Aunt Betsy seemed to listen intently, relishing every detail.

"How lovely to have such a good friend. You must never take your friends for granted, Beth. You must enjoy every single day that you have here by the lake, for you never know what the next day will bring." Betsy's eyes seemed to squint, and her hand rested for a moment on her temple, as if she were either trying to retrieve a memory or pained by one.

Suppertime at the Dobsons' was like every meal – the family sat around the table in the same designated chairs as they had at the previous meal. One of the daughters was asked to say grace – *"For what we are about to receive, may the Lord make us truly thankful."* Dishes were passed and shared. Every once in a while, between the scraping of spoon on plate, their father would remind his daughters, particularly his youngest, to keep their mouths closed while chewing. Not to hum at the table. To put down their forks and knives occasionally and "have a conversation." Zippy, trained not to beg, lay underneath the table, and was rewarded every so often with a small treat handed secretly to her.

During the meal Jean talked about a few people who had come into the store during the Sidewalk Sales – one of the Dominion Day events the merchants had planned for the weekend. In the discussion, she commented that the part-time hours in the shoe store were not enough; since she was going to university next year, she hoped to find another part-time job with hours to complement the ones she had now.

"I see in the *Reporter* where the Lakeshore Terrace is looking for extra help on Sundays, you know, to help get their big weekend smorgasbord ready. That would fit my work schedule. They always have busloads of tourists coming from Windsor and Detroit. What do you think?" she asked.

James was particularly proud of Jean's work ethic and initiative. With three daughters at home, he knew that any extra money for education could only be a good thing.

"Sounds interesting, Jean," he replied. "Why not drive over there tomorrow, or at least call and see what you can find out. Just one extra day would be enough, though. I wouldn't want you to work so hard every day that you can't enjoy your summer."

Jean nodded. James speared a piece of meat pie, put it into his mouth, and looked thoughtful.

"Lakeshore, eh? I seem to recall that a long time ago that hotel was called the Mettawas Inn. I remember when I was just a kid, Ma, Pa, Eddie, and you, Aunt Betsy, and Uncle Norman and I went to some grand opening they had there. That was a long time ago. Let's see – about the time of the First World War, I think."

Aunt Betsy put down her fork and knife and looked at her nephew at the mention of the name.

"Lakeshore Hotel, just down from the Lakeside Park," she said and sighed. "What happened to an imagination? Such names! As if you have to name a place just so people know where to find it! Now a *real* name was the Mettawas," she said, and resumed eating.

"That's a strange name, Aunt Betsy," Jean said. "Sounds Indian."

"It is, dear. Means 'where the waters come together,' I think. And your Lakeshore Terrace or Mettawas Inn is nothing compared to what the original Mettawas Hotel was like when I was a young woman. Now *that* was a grand place! A real architectural beauty that place was. Attracted all kinds of visitors. International ones, too. In fact, when I used to work there – "

At that precise moment the phone rang – two short rings – their specific call on the party line.

"Oh, hello, Jack," said James, after getting up to answer it. He listened silently for a moment or two, and then said quietly, "Much obliged, Jack. I'll be sure to tell her."

Since this was the day of the Sidewalk Sales, many of the stores had had merchandise on display for sale just outside their doors. When Jack, who owned Queen's Auto Supply across from Layman's, noticed the bench of shoes still outside the locked and darkened shoe store, he pulled the whole thing across the street to his own store and stowed them inside, bench and shoes together. Tomorrow Jean would have to collect them. He would be there early if she wanted to arrive before opening at 9 o'clock.

Jean's face registered her dismay over her carelessness.

"I can't believe I did that! I dragged that bench outside in the morning, placed the sale shoes on top, then walked inside. Out of sight, out of mind, I guess. Wow – I'll have to thank Mr. Queen for noticing and taking the time to move the shoes before they were stolen." She paused, wondered if her carelessness would cost her her job. "I wonder what Mr. Layman will say when he finds out!" she moaned miserably.

To everyone's surprise, Aunt Betsy seemed to be most

moved by the incident, and reacted strongly to Mr. Queen's thoughtful action. She cupped one hand over Jean's arm resting on the table.

"There, there, child, not to worry. No harm done. And you are so fortunate to have such a gentleman to look out for you. Perhaps you will have occasion to look out for him someday." Then she added, "That dear man always seems to know what to do and say to make me feel better...." Beth watched her sister smile in return, then look at their parents, who just shrugged in response to Aunt Betsy's confusing comment. It wasn't Jack whom Betsy was thinking about now, apparently. With the interruption, the earlier conversation about the name 'Mettawas' was forgotten by the family, but not by the old woman who sat still, pensive.

Sometimes after dinner Beth's parents would help bide the time with Aunt Betsy by playing cards. If she had a good hand, she would strum her fingers on the table and give a low, soft whistle. Today as Beth watched, the game seemed to have slowed down considerably.

"Getting tired, Auntie?" Mary asked. Beth stopped turning the pages of her Superman comic book and looked at the three of them around the kitchen table. "Auntie?" Mama repeated.

Aunt Betsy had put down her cards. The index finger of her right hand was now lightly tracing the top of her cup as she stared at the tea leaves stuck haphazardly at the bottom, read the fortune that she found there, became enthralled by their message. Beth wondered what was going on in her head at that moment, as it seemed her mother's voice must have been receding for her – just background noise to some other conversation Aunt Betsy was having inside herself at that moment.

Suddenly Betsy looked up. "I'm going to be earning some money!" she announced brightly. The excited look in her eyes announced to everyone that she was, indeed, somewhere else at that moment.

CHAPTER 8

May, 1900 – Walkerville

"Of course money is not the answer to all of life's problems, Emily – but it certainly makes sense for me to try to put some money away for the day when Norman can leave England and join me here. It's been truly lovely staying with you and Thomas these past few weeks, but I'm so anxious to find my own way," said Betsy as she folded the linen towel and laid it beside the kettle. She and her married sister had been enjoying some quiet time together for a late afternoon tea which included delicious homemade scones.

"I know you're anxious, Betsy. You're certainly a world away from home. And to top it off, leaving Norman for a new life here in Canada must have been most difficult of all."

Emily put away into the ice box the jar of her home-made peach chutney. She looked outside and caught a glimpse of her husband, Thomas, a glass maker, entering his shop that was adjacent to the brick house they had built, one of the first of its kind on Hall Avenue in the growing town of Walkerville, outside of Windsor.

"Norman says he needs to finish out the summer working on his family's sheep farm and then he can feel free to join me. We still plan to be married here next year."

Emily removed her spectacles for a moment and wiped them on her apron. Her blue eyes mirrored those of her sister's. Even without her glasses, Emily was aware of the blush on Betsy's cheeks when mentioning the young man's name. She patted Betsy's arm with affection, waiting for her to continue.

"To me the fact that Norman is a year younger than I am makes no nevermind," she said, lapsing into the familiar jargon of her family. "The dear man wants me to feel free to follow my own dreams and agreed that my leaving first was the correct thing to do. Such a departure from the other chaps we know who insist their brides remain at home at their beck and call – not that Thomas is like that either," Betsy added quickly as Emma rolled her eyes at her and sighed. The two of them left the kitchen and headed back to the dining room to finish clearing the table, Betsy's quick step easily overtaking Emily's heavier ones.

"I know, I know," Emily said, sitting down on the settee as she patted her expanding girth. "It would be ever so lovely to have a wee girl this time, but time will tell. If the next one is anything like Edward, we'll surely have our work cut out for us."

Betsy smiled, putting away the tea cosy. "You have so much to show for these last five years here, Em. When you left home we were all so sad at first – Mama most of all. She felt absolutely bereft, she told us, when you and Thomas packed the few things you had acquired together as man and wife to take up your new life in Canada.

"But we all realized – especially if one could believe the daily papers – that opportunity for young families was here. Any paper one picks up anymore back home extols the adventures and comfortable new life available for those willing to cross the seas to try and make a go of it."

She regarded the tender expression on Emily's face at the mention of their mother.

"I know you've not been home these past five years, but look at all you've gained," said Betsy as she surveyed with approval the tidy parlour just off the dining room where they were now both sitting.

"Aye, we have had our moments when money was scarce, to be sure," Emily admitted, "but now that Thomas has started his own glass company he limits the time he has to spend away from Edward and me. He finally realized that travelling on the ferry every day to work was too taxing on all of us. He also told me he had learned so much at the glass factory in Detroit and had several acquaintances there that could help him get started here. Especially with the new homes being built this side of the river.

"I tell you, dear, Walkerville and the other villages which border Windsor seem to be doing a booming business. Why, look at what that man Hiram Walker has done for us here. People still talk about him, even though he passed away last winter. He was a big American industrialist who had a hand in everything from growing crops to building his own railway.

"He's done so much for us. I've read some articles about him. You can see his influence just about everywhere, from streetlights to roads to St. Mary's Church over the way – the one he named for his wife. Even the Globe Furniture store a few blocks away is Walker's enterprise. Actually, Thomas recently received some work from them – that's how bustling a place this little village has become. Oh, and if that's not enough, one of the Detroit ferries is Walker's as well."

There was a soft stirring from little Edward upstairs. Emily looked upwards toward the ceiling, but continued her lecture.

"And the Hiram Walker's Distillery down by the river seems to be making the strongest mark around here, though I still wouldn't call him just a liquor baron, as *The Windsor Record* often does. That man has his name even on our own local newspaper. Let's see... it's around here somewhere. I've been saving these pages from the last few editions ever since I learned of your plan to settle here." She continued to rummage in the magazine rack beside the settee. "Oh – here – look at this, Betsy. Doesn't it seem as if there could be a future for you at Mr. Walker's Mettawas Hotel in Kingsville?" Emily pulled from the rack a stack of papers, and handed them to her sister.

Betsy skimmed the pages of *The Walkerville Mercury* first,

and then picked up a clipping from *The Amherstburg Echo* to read its enticing description:

Why not leave the hot and dusty city?
Come where the refreshing waters of Lake Erie
lave the beach and feet of this grand resort hotel!
Find all the comforts and luxuries of a refined
home, coupled with those outdoor amusements
which refined tastes and manners demand!

"Doesn't it sound absolutely grand?" asked Emily.

Betsy stared for a few seconds at her sensible sister who seemed almost out of breath as well as out of character. *What did she mean by encouraging her to visit such a luxurious resort when she had nary an extra penny to spend?*

"It certainly would be exciting," Betsy gently chided, "if it were not for the fact I've not the financial means to enjoy whatever this advertisement seems to promise."

"Oh my dear Betsy," said Emily, "did you think I was sending you off on holiday?" At this, Emily felt a bubble of laughter rising in her, and she wiped a tear from her eye. "Whatever are you thinking? I don't mean for you to en-joy this resort as a paying tourist. I mean for you to apply as a servant! This may be just the opportunity to make the money that you have been looking for, sister."

Suddenly, Edward's emerging wail could be heard from the nursery above. "I'll leave the papers with you to pe-ruse," Emily said with a sigh as she placed a hand on her belly and forced herself to leave the comforts of the settee.

"It sounds as if I will not get much rest after all. My little man calls." And with this, Emily left Betsy alone with her thoughts while she ascended the stairs.

The black walnut mantel clock in the parlour chimed four o'clock. Betsy poked a loosening hair pin back into her light brown hair to catch an unruly wave and keep it up and off her face. She sat down to look at the several newspapers that Emily had been collecting for her. The one on top, *The Amherstburg Echo*, caught her eye, and she proceeded to read more about the wondrous resort with the strange name.

We, the management of the Mettawas Hotel, are
desirous of securing about twenty-five or thirty
young women to be employed in the house...

Betsy closed her eyes for a moment, her thin lips pressed tightly together as she thought about her current situation. She was a single, young woman of twenty-one, and were it not for her sister and brother-in-law's generosity, she would, indeed, be alone in a new and foreign environment with no husband to provide for her and no immediate means for making her own respectable living. She dearly wanted to secure a life for herself in this area. Perhaps Norman would follow her here in a more timely fashion were her roots already planted. The longer she waited to decide, the less likely there would still be employment to be found there at the Mettawas. She would not have many days to make up her mind.

Betsy opened her eyes and slapped the paper against her hand. "I believe I'll seek my fortune at this beautiful Mettawas resort," she said to the empty room. Just as Father used to say, 'Nothing ventured, nothing gained'."

CHAPTER 9

≈

June, 1900 — Walkerville

O N A FRIDAY evening in June, Betsy anxiously await-
ed the 5:28 Mettawas Special, accompanied by Emily and her family. The young lady's nervousness was inten-
sified by the excited bustle around her at the Walkerville
Station. If the advertisements could be believed, she would
be venturing through what they beautifully described as
"sylvan and pastoral scenery." She had practically memo-
rized the wording of the enticing advertisement in *The
Amherstburg Echo* that Emily had shown her only two short
weeks ago. Much had happened since then, and now here
she was, about to open the door to a new life as one of the
twenty-five or so servants hired this summer by the management of the Mettawas Resort.

Betsy put her leather valise on the ground, repositioned
the lightweight coat on her arm, and turned to give hugs

to Emily and Thomas. She offered a fond pat on the head of her distracted little nephew who was mesmerized by the varied sights and sounds of the station. There were clip-clopping horse-drawn carriages arriving to deposit passengers, who, in turn, scurried about, secured baggage, and made tearful or cheerful goodbyes to loved ones. Some entered the stone building to pick up tickets, while others assembled on the platform. A few well-dressed couples in the latest fashion – obviously American – had just arrived from the Walker ferry, *Sappho*, having hired a carriage to bring them directly to the station. Officious looking men in uniforms carried luggage to the sleek railway cars and made conversation with each other and those around them. There was movement and noisy commotion everywhere around the one stationary beast that was the train itself.

"So, Betsy, have you got everything you need? You'll not be home this way anytime soon, you know."

Emily was assuming the role of steady, older sister, attempting calm and ease though her demeanour belied an anxiously beating heart. She would miss Betsy. The two were alone for a few minutes while Thomas had tethered his horse and carriage. They could see him approaching them now, though one of the men just off the ferry seemed to be engaged in some kind of business with him, and the two were exchanging papers.

"Oh Em, of course I have every –" but a glance at her empty hand where her pocket book should have been caused her face to flush with embarrassment. She felt a momentary jolt of panic. By now Thomas had joined them, and to him Betsy said, her voice rising, "Oh my goodness, Tom! Could you please be a dear and fetch my pocketbook? I do hope that I've left it on the seat of the buggy. My ticket is inside it!" Betsy's eyes widened as she shrugged her shoulders and looked at Emily whose face was beginning to show the strain of her toddler son, now squirming in her arms.

Ticket finally in hand, Betsy allowed Thomas to help with her suitcase to see it safely stowed in one of the railway cars. The die was cast, she thought. This fifty-minute train ride had cost her 80 cents round trip. Betsy planned to return to Walkerville in September when the Mettawas closed for the season. She would have only the weekend to learn her new responsibilities for the summer – anything from working in the kitchen, to serving in the dining room, to making up beds, to attending to one of the families as a personal nanny.

Betsy felt both trepidation and excitement as she faced the unknown. There was some pride, too, in showing some independence from her sister, and a careful optimism that began to settle on her, light as a warm, stirring breeze.

More people were arriving. Today there were only a few tourists at the station, but on Monday when the Mettawas Resort would officially open for the season, the ferry would bring more wealthy Americans, lured to Kingsville by the pamphlets which promised pampered fun and delicious cuisine in a veritable paradise on Lake Erie.

"ALL ABOARD!" shouted the conductor. "Right this

way, ladies and gentlemen!" Betsy moved in turn toward the train. There was no going back at this point.

One last wave to her only family, and then Betsy, now at the train's entrance, allowed the conductor her hand as she stepped up into the railway car. Her belongings already stowed, she had only to wend her way to a seat, preferably one by the window, she thought. Finally, she positioned herself comfortably. She removed the pin from her hat, her hat from her head, and smiled at the conductor when he came to her to request the ticket.

Beside Betsy sat a rather stocky, well-dressed gentleman whose manicured beard matched the mound of grey hair that could be seen when he had doffed his hat immediately upon entering the car. Having caught her eye, he had nodded at her in a surprisingly familiar way, asked if the seat beside her was taken, and when she replied 'no', proceeded to sit down beside her. Now Betsy gave him a sidelong glance. She noticed immediately that it was the same man who had been engaged in a conversation at the station with Thomas.

She couldn't help but build a story around him, which was something she liked to do to pass the time. She had decided that he, like her brother-in-law, was a business man. Judging from the obvious quality and cut of his suit, he must be rather wealthy. American, Betsy concluded, her head turned slightly his way as she continued to imagine the nameless man's background. Perhaps he would be travelling to Kingsville to engage in commerce with a client there. Betsy continued to allow her mind free rein. Maybe he was a widower and he would soon be enjoying a rendezvous with a lovely widow hoping to have a second chance at matrimony. She found herself smiling at her silly fantasies. The train ride continued. Betsy's eyes roved to the young red-haired woman across the aisle, sitting upright with a faraway expression on her face. Maybe she, too, might be meeting a special friend – perhaps a fiancé, Betsy thought with some guilty pleasure. This caused her to blush and she cast down her eyes to regard with some impatience her delicate hands folded on her lap. How she wished time would pass more quickly. She was anxious to wear the ring Norman promised he would put on her finger to claim her as his own. One day soon, Betsy hoped, smiling wistfully as she looked out the window. By now they had passed through an industrial area and were coursing through a rural one. She looked with interest at field after field planted with crops unidentifiable to her English eyes. The sky was a deepening blue with the occasional streak of pink and grey.

So this is the Garden of Canada that I've been reading about! Betsy could feel the gently rocking movement of the train, and hear the steadily clacking wheels rolling on steel, the occasional peal of the train whistle, the gentle murmur of voices. With eyes now closed, she heard intermittently the conductor's disembodied voice punctuating the general hum that was lulling her into a comfortable doze, every so often jostled by his sonorous announcement of another station as they came upon it. Names exotic to her and oddly European, she surmised, as she kept drifting in her thoughts.

"Pelton! Oldcastle! Paquette! McGregor! Harrow! Arner!" Then finally, "next and last stop − Kingsville station! Kingsville-on-the-Lake! Once you have disembarked, please wait inside the station until our crew can organize the valises and distribute them to their rightful owners," crowed the conductor one last time.

When Betsy stepped down from the train she smiled tentatively at the conductor to whom she proffered her hand. She smiled broadly when he said, "Enjoy your stay, Miss." She looked around her to get her bearings. Before her was a quaint fieldstone structure with an impressive slate roof and spacious portico busy with travellers. As she paused to stare at the station, someone bumped into her shoulder, causing her to stagger forward and her handbag to slip off her wrist onto the ground.

"Oh − do excuse me! How reckless of me!" said the tall, red-headed young lady Betsy had noticed sitting across the aisle from her on the train. Now she was standing at Betsy's side, a toothy grin on her face. As she bent to scoop up the purse and hand it back to Betsy, her curls fell into her eyes.

"Hello.... My name is Katherine Bethune. But my friends call me Kitty. Shall we wait over there to collect our things?"

Betsy seemed paralyzed by the unfamiliarity of everything, including the sudden appearance of this enthusiastic young girl. Noting her uncertainty, Kitty continued,

"Why don't you follow me. Have you been here before? We'll wait and collect our things over there," she was compelled to repeat.

Betsy's eyes followed the girl's outstretched arm which pointed to the covered porch on one side of the circular walkway outside the small but imposing station.

"Yes, certainly.... Hello. A pleasure to meet you. No, I haven't been here before. My apologies for looking as if I don't know what I'm doing, but to tell you the truth, I don't! I have never been to this station before," Betsy said hurriedly, looking flushed. "I'm heading for the Mettawas Resort. Do you know it? Oh, by the way, my name is Betsy. Betsy Gooding." She gingerly touched Kitty on the arm with thanks to have received the recovered handbag.

"Oh how wonderful!" answered Kitty. "I'll be heading that way as well. I'm employed there again for the summer."

The conductor and railway workers had helped the last of the passengers from the train. "If you need to enter the station, please observe that gentlemen proceed to the left, ladies to the right. If you are heading to the Mettawas, you will have a mere three blocks yet to travel down the road. Please wait in the porte-cochère for the omnibus to collect you and take you there. Enjoy your time in Kingsville, the most southerly village in British America." With a wave of his hat, he ended his rehearsed little speech and withdrew from view to help with the luggage.

A young railway worker headed in their direction with a suitcase in each of his hands. Setting them down, he winked and tipped his hat at Betsy and Kitty and said, "Please don't worry about your bags, ladies. They will magically appear with you at your final destination."

The girls looked at each other and grinned. "Well, we had better stir our stumps, then, hadn't we?" exclaimed Kitty with a laugh. "It looks as if quite a few of us are Mettawas bound," she said as she drew her arm into Betsy's and moved forward.

CHAPTER 10

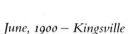

June, 1900 – Kingsville

"You say you have worked at the Mettawas before? What's it like?" asked Betsy.

Now they were milling about with the others on the
covered porch that was to one side of the station, as still
more people reunited with loved ones or waited for their
rides. There were horse-and-buggies arriving to pick up
the various passengers. Several individual horses, secured
by their reins to a steel gate on one side of the station,
stamped their feet, impatient to get on with their jobs.

It was not yet 6:30, but Betsy could feel the early evening lake breeze cooling the air, the lake less than a mile
south of where they currently stood. She drew her wrap
tightly up around her neck.

"If you're asking what the resort is like, you'll be seeing soon enough. It's just down the road right on the

water. In fact, you can just make it out if you look over there." Kitty pointed towards the south, down a maple-lined street. "The first time I saw it was last summer. I could not believe then what a fine specimen of a hotel Mr. Walker had his architects construct. Absolutely beautiful it is! Wait until you see it! But if you're asking what the job is like, I can't yet tell you. Last year I was trained in several different areas, but learned quickly enough that I was best suited for the dining area. I helped the kitchen staff when needed and served at the tables, but this year I shall be stepping up, I hope, as one of the hostesses overseeing the dining room. Excellent tip money. Those wealthy Americans certainly like to enjoy themselves!"

"Sounds promising!" replied Betsy. "Where do we stay?"

"Well, room assignments will be given as soon as we arrive. If hiring went as planned, everyone should be arriving sometime this weekend, but I'm not sure if orientation will be like last year's. You may have read where Mr. Walker passed away in the winter. With his sons in charge, I'm not certain if things will remain the same. We usually meet in the small dining room just off the main vestibule. Wait until you meet Miss Grimwood. She's our warden!"

"Warden?" Betsy felt a momentary pulse of alarm, but then saw the fun come into her new friend's eyes. "Oh – go on with you!" The two girls laughed and edged to the waiting omnibus.

Five minutes later, Betsy was in awe as she stared at the magnificent structure before her.

"My goodness, Kitty! It looks like a castle! The tourist brochures have hardly done it justice!" Betsy could feel the excitement rise in her voice.

As they disembarked from the vehicle, the girls found themselves under the carriageway portico at the main entrance hall of the Mettawas. Betsy looked up. Hiram Walker had spared no expense to ensure the enjoyment of the guests, most of whom came by rail from Detroit and by steamer from as far away as Chicago and Cleveland.

Standing outside the massive front entrance was a stern looking matron in a long-sleeved, grey dress with a fitted peplum jacket, ushering inside the group of girls around her. Her silver hair was parted in the middle and swept off her face, adding to her severe demeanour.

"Don't stand out there and gawk, girls! Make yourselves useful. Once you have identified your bag, do come inside. Come along now." Miss Grimwood turned and proceeded through the ornate lobby doors with aplomb, appropriate to her position as assistant to Mr. Matthew, the manager of the hotel. The girls fluttered behind her like ducklings following the leader. Once their load was lightened by the attendants, the greys pulling the carriage set off with a nicker down Lansdowne Avenue to return to the station.

"Set down your luggage inside the door, then, and I shall begin our tour of the main building, as well as let you have a glimpse, time permitting, of the separate entertainment facility," continued the matron. "Cook will have some strawberry scones and some cheese at the ready, I suspect."

Miss Grimwood narrowed her eyes and regarded a few

giggling girls with dawning disappointment. "After tea, I shall lay out my Rules of Decorum and we shall have a look at what is to be done before our patrons arrive on Monday. We shall all get along splendidly, as long as you abide by the rules of the house and complete your work cheerfully in a timely fashion."

From what Betsy could see, the interior of the hotel was as grand as its exterior. One could imagine how a lady and gentleman could not want for a thing here, as long as the late Mr. Walker – and now his sons – had such a magnificent vision of a luxurious and first-rate summer playground for those who could afford such trappings.

Miss Grimwood issued each girl a pamphlet of information, all the while continuing to talk. Betsy looked down at the paper in her hand. She would learn that the main hotel was built in 1889 from local field stone and had shingled gables. It was three storeys high with 133 bedrooms. The exterior certainly gave an impressive appearance. Were she to walk around the building to the lakeside, she would see seven balconies on the third floor, four on the second, and a white-columned veranda stretching across the south side, or lake side, of the building, then running the full width of the north side.

The matron's tour proceeded, and by its end, Betsy and the others who were novice servants were made aware of all the amenities the Mettawas offered. On the main floor there was a large reading room finished richly in a warm oak. The guests could relax in leather easy chairs or upholstered rocking chairs near the mammoth fireplace or write letters at dainty writing tables. There was a parlour where guests could meet other guests as they would do in their very own homes. For the gentlemen there was a smoking room. Several smaller rooms were available for guests, particularly for private parties or as play areas where children and their nannies might be seen and not heard.

A large dining room, finished in white and olive green, extended the full length of the hotel, its windows looking out at a spectacular expanse of lawn, garden, and lake. Throughout the hotel hundreds of choice paintings and engravings were distributed on the walls for the art aficionados among the guests.

"And if you look up above the dining area, girls, you will be able to see the musician's gallery, although it is somewhat difficult to see right now owing to the many beautiful plants and flowers that were installed just today. We have on the premises across the road our very own greenhouse to ensure that we always have enough blooms and tropical plants for our patrons' pleasure." Miss Grimwood seemed quite pleased with her informative lecture, though her pursed lips gave the impression she thought she might be casting pearls before swine. "Shall we venture forth outside? Come along now before it's too dark."

The girls filed out with little conversation, as the matron preferred to cut down on idle chatter. She told them how the grounds had been beautifully landscaped by a professional gardener whom Mr. Walker himself had hired from Rochester, New York. They continued down the wide walkway to the Casino.

How extensive was this tourist paradise! There was a separate building west of the main hotel which contained all the entertainment needs of the wealthy patrons, including a bowling alley, dance hall, billiard room, card room, and lounging areas. The building stood apart from the main one so that families could have privacy in the hotel, and any after-hours boisterousness could be contained. Kingsville was also a God-fearing town, so there was to be no gambling on the premises, despite the building's name of 'Casino'.

"Now, girls, shall we have a look at the entertainment building," said Miss Grimwood. Betsy found herself suddenly overwhelmed by the splendour all around – by the well-groomed paths, beautiful trees, gardens recently planted for the summer with colourful annuals of petunias, pansies, dahlias, and perennials whose names she wouldn't even recognize if she had heard them named. To one side just off this path she glimpsed a small wooden gazebo that had an unobstructed view of the harbour, a place where she imagined a couple might plan a romantic tryst.

"... also built in the Queen Anne Revival Style... two verandas from which you can see the bathing areas and..."

Betsy had already shut out the drone of Miss Grimwood's monotone. She was imagining her summer here in this magnificent environment, and then peopled her daydream with herself and her fiancé. Must she really wait until the end of summer for Norman to finally join her here? Might he be able to arrive earlier if...?

"And what say you, young lady?" The matron's abrupt

question brought Betsy back to the moment at hand, along with Kitty's firm hold on her elbow, an attempt to lead her forward. All the girls giggled and looked expectantly at the formidable presence of Miss Grimwood, who only sighed as if she had seen this dawdling before and would not tolerate it.

"If you want to have a bite to eat and still find your rooms before the night falls, you had all better get a hustle on! Morning will come very early I'm afraid, and you also have to make up your own beds before retiring for the evening."

Following a late supper in the main building, the group found itself outside the servants' quarters attached to the east end of the main hotel. "No doubt you have noticed that your group here is of the female gender," Miss Grimwood said. Several girls turned to each other to smile and comment under their breath.

She glowered and continued, "All female staff members are housed on the third floor, while on the first two floors our male staff resides. You may not under any circumstance enter these floors, nor may they visit yours. In fact, you must reach your rooms through a secure, third floor walkway which joins your quarters to the main hotel."

"Oh – the 'Bridge of Sighs'," Kitty whispered in Betsy's ear with a snicker. "Ask me later!" They both returned full attention to Miss Grimwood's Rules of Decorum.

"Fraternizing with members of the opposite... persuasion is strictly forbidden." More snickers from the girls, some biting the inside of their lips to contain their tense energy. "And there is one more thing. I should not have to tell you this, but last year I actually discovered one of my girls with contraband cigarettes; she was at her window, smoking. Nasty habit for the uncultured and uncouth. We had no choice but to have her leave immediately. So – any questions?"

All the young girls tried their best to look straight ahead and shake their heads in response.

"No? Good. Now, you will know your room by seeing your valises outside the door. Some of our male servants have already deposited them in the appropriate locations. Your door will be unlocked, the linens folded on your bed, and your room key deposited on the bedside table. You will note that two rooms share a water closet, and there is a bathing area at the end of your hall. Everyone is responsible for keeping her own area clean and tidy. I expect to see you tomorrow morning in the dining room at 6 o'clock sharp. And, oh yes, welcome to the Mettawas Resort." The girls, perhaps wondering if they had been granted permission to depart, stood their ground. "What are you waiting for? Run along!" Miss Grimwood said, and turned with a flourish.

Betsy watched Kitty enter her room down the hall with a smile and a wave, while she picked up her own suitcase and opened the door to her summer quarters. She was initially disappointed. No grand furnishings here, but a plainly appointed room with the bare necessities. She had just seen the guests' bedrooms, with the best spiral spring and hair mattresses, rich draperies on the windows, even electric bells with return call for convenience. Her single bed was made of metal, and just as the matron had said, she observed a set of sheets and a blanket folded at the foot. Fortunately the room did include a small sink and not just a washstand and pitcher. Not the comfortable lavatories of the patrons' rooms, but it would suffice.

As Betsy was just about to make her bed, a young girl with dark skin walked from the water closet on her way back to her room. She froze when she saw Betsy, whose eyes softened at the obviously gentle demeanour of the girl. She walked toward her and said, "My name is Betsy – Betsy Gooding. Looks as if we'll become quite close this summer," nodding with a grin in the direction of the water closet.

This friendly overture coaxed a smile from the girl who replied, "Hi. I'm Hattie Davis. From Harrow," she added.

After a brief conversation to learn a little about each other, the two girls parted company, each to her own room. To Betsy's surprise, when she peeked through her plain drapes and looked down below, she saw that the flower beds had been illuminated by gas lights. *No expense spared, indeed,* she thought. She was relieved to see that her room also enjoyed the incandescent electric lighting of the hotel itself. Unlike much of the rest of the village, the Mettawas offered the convenience of hot water as well as electric lights. She would be able to enjoy a bath on occasion in the small enclosed tub at the end of the hall, and then she could come in to her own little room and read at night before bed.

She saw with even more pleasure that her room was on the south side, offering a lovely view of the harbour and lake. She continued to stare out at the night. *Good time to open the window just a little to air out the room*, she thought. Through the screen she could just make out the lapping sound of the waves, and the occasional stops and starts of horse-and-buggies negotiating their way down the road. *A perfect vantage point from which to watch what might be going on down there at the harbour.* She leaned forward and saw with some fascination a dry casing of a rather large, unfamiliar insect adhering to her screen. Leaning down further to examine the thing more closely, a figure outside caught Betsy's peripheral vision. A stocky man walking away from the resort suddenly turned in her direction, looked up at her, and with a congenial wave of his hat, smiled broadly then disappeared down the sloping road that led down to the harbour. It was the very same gentleman who had sat beside her on the train.

CHAPTER 11

≈

June, 1900 – Mettawas Resort, Kingsville

B Y THE END of June, Betsy not only had familiarized herself with the place, but Miss Grimwood had noticed appreciatively her initiative and strong work ethic. As it turned out, Betsy was one of the chambermaids for the main hotel, though her responsibilities brought her also to the rooms in the Casino.

Early in the season when she had been straightening the card and billiard rooms following one of the conferences held there, she noticed that the antimacassars on the backs of lounge chairs where one's head would rest were looking rather shabby relative to the otherwise magnificent furnishings. She took one of these pieces of tatted fabric, soiled now with hair oil, soaked it in hot water, and then gave it a sound scrubbing by hand with soda crystals. *Almost good as new*, she thought, and then tended to the others. After that, Miss Grimwood permitted her to occasionally use an underused sink at the back of the kitchen when a little old-fashioned hand washing or some 'spot' cleaning would fit the bill. A little wine spill on a linen napkin. A corner of an apron sullied by brushing up against the stove. Everything had to appear as spotless as possible to meet the Mettawas standard of excellence.

Mrs. Fox, a kitchen employee who had worked at the hotel since its beginning, remembered when the hotel had laundered most of its own linen. "Those were the days of real sport, Missy, I can tell you!" Now, the Mettawas had been sending its linen and towels to the Maple Leaf Laundry in the village. Its owner, Arthur Malott, would every other day drive his horse-and-buggy to the resort to personally collect items and would return them in neatly tied parcels. He had come to know Betsy, to whom he had given some complimentary soap and soda. After all, the Mettawas had given him the bulk of his summer business.

"If the work load gets too much for you, young lady, be sure to send it my way!" he had teased one day when he had caught her gently rubbing her hands, chafed from the rubbing, pounding, and squeezing of various smaller items at the sink.

"Oh, I'm just fine for now, Mr. Malott, though I do appreciate your concern," she had said with a laugh. To herself, though, she had added the rest of her response. Why should she give up the opportunity to earn a little extra money through the tips she had received with even Miss Grimwood's sober approval? After all, now Betsy was being sought on occasion by a few older guests when they needed assistance with a last-minute laundering of a personal item or intimate undergarment. She even used the small basin in her own room at times, and spread the garment on the back of a chair often by the opened window.

Betsy had washed up at her sink and donned her maid's uniform for the day — a navy blue shirtwaist dress with a starched white apron and small cotton cap — when she was startled by the shrill whistle piercing the morning air. She had forgotten that they would be experiencing a fire drill that day.

Outside milling about were hotel patrons and servants alike. They were being rounded up by Mr. James Doan, the man elected fire chief who by day was the pharmacist in the village.

"Come away from the building if you please, ladies and gentlemen," he shouted with authority, and motioned for everyone to walk calmly and wait together by the road, while still permitting his volunteer firemen to run forward and do their work as if it were a real emergency.

By now, Kitty had joined Betsy and drew her aside. "Don't you just love a man in uniform?" she exclaimed with a giggle, pointing to the men who were identifiable as a real fire fighting team with their bold red shirts and blue trousers. It was a fact in the village that the best equipment belonged to Hiram Walker and Sons. Their pumping station down the hill from the hotel made it easy for Walker to have built underground waterlines. Just a few years ago he had twenty-seven fire hydrants installed to assure the safety and protection of his assets. This was the Mettawas team of firemen who had done their best a mere two years ago in a real emergency to assure that Mr. Malott's laundry would not succumb to fire. Their superior hook and ladder outfit, chemical fire engine, and new hose carts had been able to save the laundry equipment, much to Mr. Malott's appreciation, allowing his Maple Leaf Laundry to be relocated on Division Road.

Hattie came up to her two friends and the three girls surveyed the scene before them.

Suddenly, one of the hotel workers approached them. "Just got this Kodak for my birthday," he said. "First in my family to own one! May I take your picture? Something for all posterity," he added with a grin. Betsy put her arm around the waists of her two companions to accommodate the request.

"Now when you're rich and famous from these photographs, be sure to acknowledge how beautiful the subjects are!" Kitty said.

"Do you think I may have a copy when you have your pictures developed?" Betsy asked.

After the drill, one of the young men named Danny turned with a broad grin in Kitty's direction. He knew better than to converse with the fire chief looking on, but he knew he would be approaching this lovely red-haired lady again sometime. When Kitty turned to look at him, she smiled, and then broadened that smile in recognition. Here was the young man at the train station who had assisted Betsy and her with their bags when they had arrived a mere two weeks ago.

After the day's chores, Betsy was walking by the kitchen where she glanced at Kitty depositing a tray piled high with dirty dishes. They waved at each other. She knew her friend had been disappointed that she had not received the enviable role of dining room hostess, but Kitty was the kind of girl who could make the best of any situation. Her outgoing personality was put to other good use. When she was not busy attending to the patrons in the dining area, she was often seen helping nannies occupy the small children in the playroom to give exhausted mothers and fathers a well-deserved break.

Kitty had not been the only one who had met disappointment at the hotel this summer. Times were changing, a few of the older employees like Mrs. Fox had said, from the days when Mr. Walker was around.

"Was a time when Mr. Hiram Walker himself would come by and personally say a few words to everyone who worked here. And he liked to give a sizeable bonus to anyone who seemed to go above and beyond," she had said to Betsy one time when both were at one of the sinks in the kitchen.

Now, it seemed that more was being asked of the help. Little by little it was becoming obvious that the services offered and conditions experienced at the resort were meeting the strict hand of a management showing signs of financial distress while still striving to deliver the best.

Betsy was philosophical when Miss Grimwood asked

her to help distribute the flowers to various rooms and arrange them in vases, as an extension of her chambermaid's duties. This extra responsibility turned out to be one she greatly enjoyed, because it allowed her the freedom to leave the confines of the hotel itself and venture outside to the hotel's own greenhouse across the road. She always relished time to reflect on her life in Kingsville. A life she hoped to build with Norman one day.

As she looked outside toward Park Street, she caught a glimpse of the congenial, debonair man who had sat beside her on the train that day when they had arrived at the resort from Walkerville. Now she knew his name – Mr. Wallace. Today he was alone, though often he was seen in the company of a burly, uniformed man walking a little black dog.

In the beginning of her stay at the Mettawas she had been curious as to why she had seen him striding with purpose everywhere – down the hotel corridors, walking through the Casino's smoking or billiard rooms, pacing hither and yon through the various gardens, chatting with the guests in the dining area – so she had come right out and asked him. Surprised, yet delighted with the young lady's candid inquisitiveness, he had explained his job at the hotel. He had been retained by Hiram Walker to keep watch and ward over persons and property. It was his job to oversee all day-to-day activities at the resort, including the quality of services the patrons had learned to expect. More importantly, however, he was hired to be a trouble-shooter for the establishment as well, for it was his job to intervene if guests became too boisterous, or if anyone acted untoward.

During the first year of the hotel's existence, several waiters had been a source of annoyance to the law-abiding citizens of Kingsville. When people would walk down Park Street, past the resort, these wayward employees had been outside, tossing vile and slanderous remarks at them, as a lark.

In those early days of the hotel's existence, Mr. Walker had hired mostly Americans to work at the hotel. When he had heard some of the people from the village were afraid to venture by the buildings after nightfall, Mr. Walker immediately sent those scamps on the next train back to Detroit, Mr. Wallace had explained to Betsy in an earlier conversation. After that, he hired more local people who, he thought, might take a different attitude toward their fellow citizens.

"Mr. Walker worked hard, had a strong moral character, and demanded no less from his employees, while at the same time he was always mindful of being fair to them as well. To us." Mr. Wallace's voice had risen, but the last words seemed to stick in his throat. When they had that conversation, Betsy could see that he had great admiration for the man. He had continued to explain the eventual hiring of the night watchman.

"So after that first year, Mr. Walker hired another man, Terrence – the chap you often see on the grounds walking his little black dog. He helps me keep peace here at the Mettawas. I guess you could say that while I'm the communicator, Terrence is the enforcer," he added with a chuckle.

Communicator he was indeed. Originally hired by Mr. Walker himself, it was no secret that Mr. Wallace had been on several occasions critical of the way the Walker sons were executing their roles following the death of their father. It had begun with Mr. Walker's stroke five years before when he had conferred on his sons more responsibility. Sadly, Mr. Walker had not always approved of their financial prowess, though he had still made his son Harry the treasurer of the Company overseeing the Mettawas. While they supervised the financial output and intake, they didn't seem to have the same emotional investment in Kingsville that their father had. They spent little time in the cottages that their father had built for them, and seemed uninterested in pursuing his dream of building more cottages on the shores of Lake Erie.

Though Mr. Wallace had not said it in so many words, Betsy had the impression that the man greatly missed old Mr. Walker and had even referred to him as "Hiram" at times. He had reminisced with real fondness that the older man had treated him like a son, and had always made him feel that his opinion was one he respected, even sought on occasion. Wallace couldn't say that the sons treated him like a brother because they certainly did not. Looking into their circle from outside, he could see that little by little they were divesting themselves of their land and holdings here in Kingsville. And why should they have any time for him, after all, for they would have thought of him merely

as one of their many employees. Betsy had heard him
more than once grumble about the resort's future; he complained about matters she knew or cared little about: profit
loss and bottom lines and tax breaks. From what Betsy had
heard, there were others among the staff who had worked
there over a decade now also holding out hope that when
the subject of tax assessments came up at the next council
meeting early in July, there would be a favourable outlook
for the Mettawas.

Both Betsy and Mr. Wallace arrived at the greenhouse
at the same time. He quickly doffed his hat and nodded in
her direction. From his waistcoat pocket she could see the
glint of the gold chain of his watch.

"Why, good evening, Miss Gooding! Are you here to
collect a few posies for the rooms?"

"Yes, sir," Betsy replied. "I shan't be staying in there too
long, though – too humid for me." She self-consciously
tucked under her cap a few escaping tendrils with one
hand, and smoothed the front of her apron with the other.

Mr. Wallace smiled at her in response. "Ah yes! These
summer days by the lake seem heavy enough with the
day's humidity, wouldn't you say? One needs only to walk
in the evening down by the harbour to freshen up one's
dampened spirits!"

"Quite! I often sit by my window at night when I
can't sleep. There's almost always a beautiful breeze waft-
ing through, even when the day has been unbearable with
the heat. Why I can see so much from there! On clear
nights I've counted six lighthouses visible, including the

one they call the 'Dummy Light' beyond what I'm told is called 'Pointe au Pelée'. Sometimes I even see you all alone late evening walking down toward that squat little building with the tall brick chimney. You know – the water-pumping station, I think. In fact..."

Mr. Wallace blanched at Betsy's admission of watching him walk alone on the grounds at night, especially his late night sojourns down the sloping path leading toward the harbour.

He took his watch from his pocket, looked at it with a frown, and said somewhat abruptly, "Well, I should permit you to go about your business, Miss Gooding, and I'll continue with mine. Enjoy what's left of the day."

As she watched him politely nod in her direction and open the door for her, then stride quickly away, she wondered why he suddenly seemed ill at ease. Next time she would try to find an opportunity to ask. For now, though, she would collect several fresh bouquets of lilacs and return to the hotel.

No sooner had she entered the building when Miss Grimwood came up to her, out of breath. "Your sister in Walkerville would like you to return her call, Miss Gooding. She says it's urgent. I believe you already have her number," she added. Betsy wasn't sure if there were a note of disapproval in Miss Grimwood's voice or not, but she thanked her and proceeded to the telephone in the main lobby of the hotel.

The Mettawas had been one of the first subscribers to Bell Telephone Company and had several telephones available for its many American patrons. The households in the village rarely had a telephone, though this was just beginning to change with some of the merchants requiring one in their stores. Since Emily had access to her husband's business phone in his Walkerville glass shop, the two sisters had already availed themselves of the luxury.

As it turned out, the call would bring a smile to Betsy's face. Norman had left England earlier than he had expected, Emily had explained. He would now be arriving in Canada sometime early July, and he would make his way to Walkerville where he would find free room and board with Emily and her husband. Thomas could use an extra hand in the shop, and that would help Norman land on his feet in his new life here. If all went well, by summer's end he could have the resources to join her in Kingsville. Thomas had said that there was a glass factory in Kingsville, too, if Norman took to the work, or perhaps he would find another calling. In any event, Betsy's joy knew no bounds; her future was looking bright.

After Betsy had returned to place bouquets in a few rooms, she soon found herself outside Mrs. Rankin's room, toward which the prim and proper old lady was walking, husband in tow, having returned from their dinner downstairs.

"Good evening, Ma'am," Betsy said. "I hope I'm not disturbing you, but I would like to exchange these flowers for the tired-looking ones in your room. I'll be only a moment."

"Thank you, young lady. By the way, I didn't thank you

properly for washing the coffee stains from my husband's brand new tie." She looked askance at her husband who just shrugged and looked either apologetic or bored – Betsy wasn't sure which – and then opened her pocketbook, fished out a twenty-five cent piece, and handed the coin to Betsy. Though civil, she had never learned Betsy's name; to her she was just the laundress with the English accent, someone to command, as Mrs. Rankin was wont to do.

"I also have another little job for you, if you would be so kind." As they entered the room, she walked to the closet and pulled off the hanger a fashionable French batiste gown in soft blue pastel. Betsy's eyes widened at the sheer beauty of it, though Mrs. Rankin cast it toward her as if it were a mere distasteful rag. "It seems to have a ring of face powder around the collar and I would like to wear it to the dance on the weekend. I was hoping that you could spot clean it?"

The walk back to her room with the dress over her arm made Betsy smile. With the extra money she had been making, she could now afford a new shirtwaist, or perhaps even those Empress shoes which were advertised on sale at Scratch's in the village. The One Price House also offered white cotton skirts this week for $1.95. With the heat and wear and tear on her clothes, she already felt the need to refresh and lighten her summer wardrobe.

It was during these thoughts that Betsy heard her grumbling stomach and realized she had not gone in to the servants' small dining area for supper. She wished she could just take some bread and cheese out on the lawn and have her own little picnic, but she knew that management had discouraged the help from − as they had put it − 'loitering' around under the noses of their paying guests.

Kitty was still inside the hotel, cleaning up from dinner and helping to set the tables for breakfast. No doubt she would try to join Betsy and the others later in the evening in their rooms when they could share the day's stories and gossip, and end the day with a good belly laugh. Betsy liked those times best, and was grateful for the few close friends she had now − friends she hadn't even known existed a mere two weeks ago.

By now she had left the main hotel and was walking across the third floor walkway leading to the girls' dormitory − a walkway the locals called the 'Bridge of Sighs'. As promised, Kitty had explained the meaning for the name one night when the two of them had stood in the corridor, looking through the windows to see several young men standing outside on the ground waving up at them. They could look up at the young women, but couldn't get to them; the girls were safely out of the reach of any pining suitor below.

When Norman arrived shortly − *could he really be arriving by the end of next month?* − she would have so much to share with him, she thought dreamily. Right now she gazed through the window, turning her face upward to the sky already showing the beginning streaks of dusk. Her face, pale and delicate when she had arrived mid-June, was now glowing with health from the sun. Though every day seemed to shimmer with heat, she could already feel the cooling lake breeze that she knew would await her tonight at her bedroom window.

It never ceased to amaze Betsy when she regarded the map of the Dominion of Canada that she was living in the most southerly part of the country. In a couple of hours the sun would slide down the blue depth of sky, leaving streaks of rose, orange, and gold. *"Red sky at night, sailors' delight,"* she had learned to say when the sun set spectacularly. The full moon over the lake that week had been equally stunning, as the waves capped in white froth by day seemed often tamed at night by the white orb above them.

I could certainly come to love this place of beauty and change, Betsy thought. The best part of all was the realization that with the following day being Sunday, she had the morning free to worship along with the other servants at their church of choice, and following the service was the picnic at Paradise Grove, sure to be an adventure, indeed.

CHAPTER 12

≈

June, 1900 – Mettawas Resort, Kingsville

KITTY HAD ASKED Betsy to attend the service at Epworth Methodist Church on Division Road, the church that was either a long walk or a short buggy ride from the Mettawas. This Sunday the girls were fortunate to have been offered a ride there, the better option since the dusty roads could sully their Sunday attire. As they alighted from the carriage, young Danny, the lad they had seen at the fire drill earlier in the month, was approaching the church from Mill Street where he had locked his bicycle near the livery stable used by the church congregation. He was delighted to see them.

"Good morning to you, Miss Bethune, Miss Gooding! It's so lovely to see you both out to church!"

Betsy and Kitty looked at each other with a giggle, well aware that the young man's gaze had fallen upon their ankles, made bare by skirts swishing in the morning breeze. With one white-gloved hand each girl held her hat in place, and with the other, clutched a pocketbook in which there was a small envelope with a little offering for the collection plate. Danny held the heavy wooden door of the church open for them to pass through first.

"Yes, well Danny, so good to see you out of your fireman's togs – I mean – oh you know what I mean," Kitty said with a blush on her cheek and a twinkle in her eye when she saw the young man's amused reaction. Danny fell into step behind them as the three entered the church.

After the service, Betsy and Kitty planned to walk back to the hotel in order to collect the basket of strawberry custard tarts that the chefs, Margaret and Peter, had allowed them to take as their contribution to the picnic at Paradise Grove. They relished this time to catch up with each other's news, and on the return trip were less worried about a little mud on their shoes or hem. On the way home, Danny passed them on his bicycle, waving his hat at them and saying, "See you ladies in Paradise!" With a chuckle, Kitty finally confided in Betsy that the two had started to see each other once they had met at the fire drill two weeks ago. Danny volunteered as a fireman, but his main employment was as a ticket seller at the train station. His optimistic spirit seemed indomitable, and Betsy approved of him as a fitting match for the fun-loving Kitty.

The walk home turned to the morning's sermon. "What did you think of the Reverend Mr. Hamilton's warning against "outside agents" who have the potential to destroy the "moral fabric of our village," as he put it?" Betsy asked, as she waved at the driver of a carriage turning down Wigle Street.

"Well, it seems obvious to me that many of the comments were directed against the Walkers whom I've heard some of the people on the village council see as mere liquor barons. People are wary of the wealthy Americans who come here in droves during the summer, but then disappear in the winter. 'Beware the green-eyed monster,' you know. I'm sure there's a bit of envy when the locals compare their horse-and-buggies to those elegant carriages that are seen down by the Mettawas." Kitty quickened her step, having bypassed a large rut in the road, and now linked her arm in Betsy's.

"But why the fire and brimstone? Surely the village must see that these same wealthy people occasionally patronize their stores, and therefore bring money to the merchants," Betsy continued. "Why, just the other day I overheard one of our guests talking about the new clothing items she had purchased on sale in the village shops."

"I guess it's just human nature to be suspicious of the unknown, and remember, the good ladies and gentlemen of the congregation rarely know what goes on at the hotel. All they know is that there is usually quite a bit of ruckus that they hear coming from the grounds and lake. You should hear what Danny tells me," Kitty said with a knowing air. "He sees and hears quite a bit, working as he does at the station. Some people complain that these rich Americans seem to do nothing but play! They see them in their fancy carriages, and they assume they eat decadent meals at the hotel and drink too much Canadian Club, that they dance every night to the hotel's very own orchestra, and play games every day on the lawn. He actually overheard a conversation between two old ladies who suspected that some people were even bathing on Sundays! In bathing costumes that actually bared too much of their bodies, they complained! Heaven forbid!" Kitty said with a laugh, her explanation of the real and imagined debaucheries of the resort causing Betsy to grin in response.

After their political and moral musings, they turned the discussion to matters of the heart and their respective boyfriends, and then, finally, to the day's picnic.

Paradise Grove was a clean, first-class picnic ground about a mile west of the village. It was Hiram Walker who several years before had relocated the Grovedale Tabernacle there, which had been adjacent to his Mettawas property and had been used for various public meetings. He had felt this building would be put to better use in a more public area. Walker had fitted the park with every outdoor convenience and had encouraged those from neighbouring communities to enjoy it; Walker's trains would stop at the Grove to let off and take on excursionists.

Once back at the hotel, Betsy and Kitty were en route to the kitchen to collect their basket of sweets. The tables were being set for an early Sunday dinner, as expected. What else caught their eyes and ears alarmed them. Mrs. Rankin and Miss Grimwood were engaged in an animated conversation just outside the dining room. The hotel guest did not look pleased. She was gesturing in their direction now that they had entered the area, talking with great animation, and though the girls could not hear what she was saying, they knew the words were not making Miss Grimwood very happy. She turned toward them and seemed to frown in Betsy's direction.

"Oh no," Betsy said half under her breath. "I hope she hasn't disapproved of the few phone calls I've made to my sister in Walkerville."

At that point Mrs. Rankin turned on her heel and left the room. Miss Grimwood was approaching Betsy who leaned into Kitty to say, "If you can just collect our basket of sweets, I'll stay and see what Miss Grimwood wants. I'll meet you in our hallway at quarter past the hour. Uh... if you don't find me there you had better send out the cavalry," she said, trying to make light of what was becoming a tense situation.

"A word, please, Miss Gooding," the matron said as she approached Betsy.

"Good day, Ma'am," Betsy said with a quick curtsy. Her anxiety was causing her to crush her Sunday church hat that she held in one hand.

"I was wondering whether you have seen Hattie today." Betsy shook her head.

"Well, once you return to your quarters, see if she is in her room. Send her to me, please, as soon as possible. I need to speak to her about a very serious matter."

"Certainly, Ma'am," said Betsy, and then stood for several seconds in place as she watched the woman's retreating back. She expected to see Hattie later at the picnic since several congregations were coming together to enjoy the usual rousing speeches and the delicious meal that the ladies of each church would provide. Hattie would no doubt be there with her other coloured friends, including her new beau, Aaron.

"Oh dear, Hattie," Betsy asked herself, "what have you got yourself into?"

Upstairs she found Kitty whose interest in the situation quickly waned once she knew that her friend had no real details. Worse, Hattie was not in her room, and had no doubt left directly with friends from the little church in Salem. That was a small rural community just beyond the village where the white and coloured people lived affably together, though their places of worship and schooling were separate.

Outside was the usual commotion – both gentlemen and ladies on bicycles on the road and sidewalk, often to the disgruntlement of carriage drivers working to keep their horses calm and focussed. Though Betsy had not been a proficient cyclist before the summer, she was quickly learning that this mode of transportation was both pleasurable and practical. Today Kitty and she had been given permission to borrow two of the hotel's bicycles. With the strawberry treats contained in Kitty's bicycle basket, the two were soon wending their way to Paradise Grove.

The afternoon of gold sun and green space played out beautifully. Young boys dressed in shorts with long stockings pulled up to their knees and white caps on their heads played a game of tag, or threw a ball to each other, or chased little squealing girls dressed in dainty gingham frocks. Some children pushed each other on the wooden swings, calling out in delight to each other. Not one was heeding maternal admonitions to try to stay clean. Since it was Sunday and bathing was prohibited, the older girls and boys leisurely walked together through the groves of trees, the young ladies twirling parasols to protect them from the sun.

By mid-afternoon all of the men and most of the women had found their way to the tabernacle. Betsy and Kitty, having decided that they had heard enough lectures for one day, decided to help the women who had stayed back by the picnic tables. They were putting away the remnants of the shared feast, wiping sticky fingers and faces of their small children, gossiping about people and places and some of the changes and events in the village.

There was no doubt that the village was growing; in fact, there was talk that by next year at this time it might even achieve town status. There was also much discussion about the new merchants establishing their businesses on Main, and about council making improvements to the roads and sidewalks.

"About time!" said one who had just secured the lid on what was now an empty biscuit tin. "I hope they plan to put up some light at Division and Park. It's such a dangerous bend in the road at night, what with the Mettawas just around the corner."

"Speaking of the Mettawas," said another, "my niece

works there, and she told me the funniest story. While sweeping out the bathing house down there at the beach, she said a female guest approached her, asking how far it would be to walk to Muskoka because she and some friends wanted to visit someone there that afternoon! Imagine!"

The women around her laughed and shook their heads in disbelief at the folly no doubt to be found at the Mettawas. Betsy and Kitty were beginning to regret that they had chosen to help clean up the tables rather than hear the more political talk in the tabernacle.

"Well, I know several of the tourists who have stayed at the Mettawas, and they are absolutely polite and civil and no problem at all," said yet another of the women. "To tell you the truth, I think any problem starts with the people in charge of the place. They seem to want everything to be so perfect for their guests that they can't abide any outsiders walking on the property or using what they see as their very own sand beach. Maybe they don't realize how fortunate they are to have the best views of the lake around here."

Her friend nodded in agreement. "It's true that the management seems to want the best of the best. But what about the fact that they can bend the law? Why, my son Jimmy last spring was stopped by a constable and fined for riding his bicycle on the sidewalk. He was pretty angry when he returned home, complaining about how in the summertime the constables look the other way when everyone down by the Mettawas rides on the sidewalks.

Different rules, I guess, depending on money," she added with a sniff of disdain.

Betsy and Kitty looked at each other, and then glanced over at the tabernacle. Had they left the gossiping women and walked into the tabernacle, they would have heard the Reverend Mr. Hamilton, the outgoing minister of the Epworth congregation, speaking about their community spirit which had made him feel so welcomed when he had first arrived at Epworth. That spirit was obvious in the coming together of the area congregations that very day, he had said. He reminded everyone not only of the importance of community, but of the necessity of patriotic duty; one had only to open the weekly *Reporter* to read about what was happening in Pretoria and the Boer War and the heroic actions of our British troops, as he reminded them. Of course, they all expressed their pride in the five local boys who had volunteered to fight as part of the Canadian contingent on behalf of the Motherland. The rousing speech was a fitting end to a glorious afternoon of excess – in food, fun, and fellowship.

By later afternoon, Betsy, Kitty, and Danny had returned from the picnic, their youthful exuberance dulled only slightly by energy spent and food consumed. The young man lingered in his goodbye to his girl, whose cheeks were glowing from both sun and adoration. Betsy bid them both farewell and returned to the servants' annex. What worried her was Hattie's absence; she had not seen her at the picnic after all.

But when Betsy returned to her room, she heard Hattie

crying inside the locked water closet. Moments later, the young chambermaid emerged looking dishevelled, eyes bloodshot, cheeks wet from tears.

"My heavens, Hattie, whatever is wrong?" Betsy said, moving toward her friend and putting an arm around her shoulders. It took several minutes for the girl to compose herself long enough to attempt an explanation for her unhappiness.

"I can't believe it! I returned here following church today, and Miss Grimwood caught me before I was able to leave for the picnic. She was so cross with me, Betsy! She told me that Mrs. Rankin has accused me of stealing her ruby earrings! Betsy, I've never seen her earrings, let alone touched any of her jewellery. But since she knows I clean her chamber, she assumes that I must be some kind of thief!" Hattie sat down, head in both hands as the tears continued to roll down her face.

After assuring Hattie that she believed she was telling the truth, Betsy was able to calm her finally and help her get ready for bed. Most certainly Mrs. Rankin was mistaken, she had said to Hattie, and the earrings would surface, probably by tomorrow. But the next day the jewellery remained missing, Mrs. Rankin accusatory, and Hattie steadfast in her innocence.

The routines of the coming week continued, each day rolling into the next. Hattie would have lost her job entirely if not for the fact there was no evidence that she was the thief. Still, the beautiful ruby earrings were nowhere to be found. Miss Grimwood had even searched Hattie's room and belongings. More humiliation followed for Hattie with the obvious gossip among the guests which took on a life of its own. Hattie felt that they were looking at her differently, that her behaviour was under scrutiny – behaviour of a *coloured* maid, she had heard them say behind her back. "Whom could you really trust after all?" a few of the patrons had asked.

Owing to the growing distrust felt by such valued regular customers, Hattie was no longer allowed in the hallways of the hotel, and the rooms that she cleaned and tidied were confined to the Casino only. Miss Grimwood reluctantly had to tell her that by the weekend she would likely be dismissed, even if the earrings had not been found in Hattie's possession. After all, the Mettawas had its reputation to uphold. The guests had to feel that while on the Mettawas grounds their treasured property was secure. Betsy remembered when she had put fresh flowers in the Rankins's room, and the several times she had let herself in to leave the laundered 'unmentionables'. *Funny*, she mused, *Hattie was not the only person with access to these rooms, but she alone has been accused.*

Curiously, there was a difference in attitude toward Hattie depending on whether one was a guest or an employee, particularly a servant from Kingsville. The local white people were not so quick to judge her. Apparently their experience of having 'Old Wash' in their midst tempered the regard they had toward coloured people. Henry Washington claimed to be over a hundred years old, and seemed generally to love people. He would walk down

Main Street wearing his shabby brown robe, telling people their fortunes in exchange for food. And he loved his reputation as a successful matchmaker. It was he who had introduced Hattie to Aaron Henderson, a farmer out in Salem. Even the local children loved to sit together in a circle around Old Wash and hear his many stories of adventure. Nevertheless, when he had been walking around Park Street outside the Mettawas, several of the American guests had complained to the management. Rumour was circulating among them that now there was a thief in their midst as well. "Can't trust any of those coloureds!" Betsy had heard some guests say.

Betsy was about to return to the servants' annex, having just collected yet another item from Mrs. Rankin to spot clean, although it galled her to do so. Mr. Wallace had come around the corner and the two almost collided. He had proven from their first conversation to be a good friend to her, a kind of father figure who listened carefully to her concerns and usually gave her good-natured advice. It was he who recommended she call her sister when she felt lonely. Whenever a young man flirted with her, Mr. Wallace would warn the daring lad that she was 'taken' by a beau who would be arriving there soon – a tall, strapping fellow who would give anyone a sound comeuppance if he persisted in annoying the lovely Miss Gooding! This always made Betsy laugh, and yet she appreciated his concern for her well-being. It especially made her smile to herself, remembering that the "tall, strapping" fiancé of hers was rather short in stature, though tall in spirit.

"Hello, Miss Gooding – did you have a profitable day today?" he asked, nodding at the packet in her hand. "What are you up to this evening – another interesting sporting adventure? Perhaps a bicycle ride with Miss Bethune, your tireless companion?" Mr. Wallace smiled at the memory of the two young women several days ago when they had decided to ride bicycles the hotel kept strictly for the guests. Kitty had taken off down the road with a laughing Danny riding beside her, and had not seemed to care that the dour-faced Miss Grimwood who had been watching from the hotel's entranceway was not amused. Betsy, though willing to try to ride, had found her skirts becoming cumbersome and the handlebars difficult to steady, throwing her off balance. She had stopped too suddenly, and the bicycle, like a bucking horse, had forced her to fall. Fortunately she had not been riding very quickly, and there were no broken bones, only bruised pride. "Absolutely inappropriate behaviour," Miss Grimwood had taken them aside to say afterward, in addition to the reprimand for unauthorized use of resort property.

Betsy flushed at the memory. "Ah – go on with you, Mr. Wallace – can't a girl have a little fun?"

"Well, if it be fun that you're looking for, young lady, I suggest that you wait for your lad to arrive. You'll want to be in one piece!" They both shared a laugh at Betsy's expense as they walked together down the corridor and out the door into the beautiful grove of trees outside the hotel.

Betsy pointed to a path disappearing down the terraced lawn leading to the harbour below. "I've seen you walk down there countless times, Mr. Wallace. What's the big attraction down at the docks in the evening?" Betsy asked.

"What – besides the cool breezes? I told you that I love in the quiet of an evening to hear my heels click against the wooden pier, to smell the fish being hauled from the fishing boats, to see the foam on the water, to hear the calls of seagulls...." Mr. Wallace lit his pipe, his mouth twisted in a stifled laugh. Betsy was no threat to him, and he knew it. He also knew the girl was worried about her friend, Hattie, so he deflected interest in his whereabouts by appealing to Betsy's concern for her friend.

"Say – how is the poor Hattie Davis faring these days? I've heard she has had a tough go of it."

"That is precisely the matter I wanted to discuss with you, Mr. Wallace. You always seem to know what to say, and these days, I hardly know how to talk to the poor lass. She's quite beside herself, and with good reason. I have no idea what has happened to those earrings, but I can tell you with confidence, I believe Hattie when she tells me she had nothing to do with them. She is most definitely not a thief," Betsy stated emphatically. She continued, "I consider it a travesty that the girl has been considered guilty already – why, rumour has it that she shall be asked to leave the Mettawas by the end of the week. Many of the guests apparently do not want her in their rooms! Her reputation has been sullied, and it is grossly unfair. I would trust Hattie with my life, I can tell you! And her family desperately needs that money she contributes weekly!" Betsy's face flushed hot with the memory of her friend's situation.

"I'm not certain I can tell you what to say to your poor friend," Mr. Wallace said, "but I'm sure I don't really have to. Your kind feelings toward her are all the support she needs. She feels your concern. I'm most certain of it." Betsy smiled in appreciation of his comments.

"Still – let me think on this for a moment. I know that the hotel has overbooked its guests for the month of July, especially with the upcoming Dominion Day festivities. The first two floors of the residence reserved for the male help are going to be required for some additional room assignments for guests, believe it or not! Management will need a capable person who knows the routines around here to help arrange those rooms for new tenants. If Hattie were to help clean not only the rooms in the Casino, where I believe she is working now, but also the two lower floors in the residence, then she can avoid the main hotel and those old gossips altogether."

The knot in Betsy's brow was beginning to ease.

Mr. Wallace continued, "I know for a fact that our overbooked status is a double-edged sword. Of course, the treasurer is ecstatic – Heaven knows the Mettawas needs the money – but management is scrambling to accommodate the extra clientele. I shall speak to Miss Grimwood about the necessity of keeping our young Miss Hattie, and together we can approach hotel management. We all know what a wonderful worker the girl really is."

"Oh, thank you, Mr. Wallace! Might I be permitted to raise her spirits and tell her of the possibility of work in the residence, such as you have described?"

"Best not to say anything specific as yet, my dear. Suffice it to say that there are friends in high places who have taken her situation to heart and are working on her behalf."

"There you go, Mr. Wallace! I just knew you would be able to figure a way to get to the light of this otherwise dark tunnel!" Betsy threw her arms quickly around the man's broad shoulders, then realizing where she was and with whom, withdrew and said more soberly, "You're a wonderful friend, Mr. Wallace. And to think that I have just made your acquaintance this summer!"

She paused for a moment. "Goodness! I forgot to ask – what about all those workers who will be displaced by the guests taking over their rooms?"

"That's the double-edged sword, Miss Gooding, as we are scrambling to billet the workers in nearby homes. Actually, most have been accounted for already, thanks to the goodwill of many of our Kingsville neighbours."

After bidding each other a "good evening", Betsy turned to retrace her steps and wend her way back to the hotel, where she would take the indoor corridor – the 'Bridge of Sighs' – which led to the third floor ladies' quarters. That night she, Kitty, and Hattie had a good talk, and she knew that her beleaguered friend was now feeling less alone.

Betsy mulled over much of what Mr. Wallace had said earlier in the evening. First of all, she was excited about the real possibility of her friend keeping the job which she so very much needed. Second, she was selfishly grateful that she and her friends on this floor were not being displaced by this "overbooking". Third, she thought for a long time about what Mr. Wallace had described as the "goodwill" of their Kingsville neighbours.

Human nature is odd and unpredictable, was all that she could conclude. On the one hand, she had heard comments last Sunday about the moral fabric of the village being torn asunder by the Mettawas, and on the other hand, there were these kind people in the village who were coming to the aid of the management by billeting complete strangers in their own homes. *Strange,* Betsy thought as she was putting on her night attire. *I shall never understand human nature if I live to be a hundred.*

She turned out the light in her little sanctuary and walked to her window, opening it more than she usually did at night. There was almost no breeze at all; the drapes fell stock still, not a free breath of air to be had. There was no moon, but the illumination of the Mettawas gardens highlighted a dog walking beside two men, keeping watch over people and property, just as Mr. Wallace had assured her.

CHAPTER 13

≈

July, 1900 – Mettawas Resort, Kingsville

SUMMER WAS PROMISING to be lovely and hot. June had brought little rain, and now that July had begun, the leisurely, sunny days continued to be perfect for bathing in the lake, meandering through the grove of trees and flower beds, or taking part in one of the several sports available at the resort: golf at the Mettawas Links, tennis at one of its courts, horse riding from its nearby stable, bicycle jaunts into the village – all part of the resort's many outdoor activities.

Indoors was bustling as well. Nannies, busy with their little charges, sometimes appeared just outside the kitchen for a small bucket of ice chips to attend to a scraped knee or swollen elbow. The Mettawas kitchen always had enough ice, even in the hottest summers. Ice chunks, cut from the frozen lake in the winter, were hauled to the ice house in town behind Grenville's ice cream parlour by workers hired by the resort. This was preferable to what some individual homesteads had to do, which was to bury the ice underground and cover it with sawdust from the local mill. In the summer months the ice needed at the Mettawas was taken from the ice house and stored in a huge ice chest in the middle of the kitchen.

The kitchen and dining areas were particularly busy given the next day's schedule of Dominion Day activities. In honour of the occasion, the railway rates would be reduced so the Mettawas could expect additional guests. All the area hotels anticipated an increase in the number of mouths to feed and the kitchens were especially hectic.

Dominion Day was the July holiday when people could express their pride in Canada and her role in the Commonwealth. Tomorrow there would be a grand parade with marching bands from Main Street to Paradise Grove, where hundreds would assemble to hear rousing speeches in the tabernacle, draped with red, white, and blue, and where people would flock from Windsor and its border cities to enjoy their family picnics. There would be sailboats on the water, swimmers of all shapes and sizes costumed in their acceptable flannelette, and various sporting events for everyone to enjoy. Not only were more guests expected at the Mettawas, but special meals would be offered at all the area hotels. In the evening there would be a concert in the town hall. There might not be quite the same enthusiasm as there was for Victoria Day in late May when the whole village wrapped itself in bunting and waved both the Union Jack and British Red Ensign, but the Dominion Day holiday was becoming increasingly popular, particularly among the young people.

Walker and Sons had traditionally provided the prizes for these events and this year was no exception. There would be a bicycle race from the village to Ruthven and a baseball match between Kingsville and Amherstburg on the Mettawas lawn early in the afternoon. At 5 o'clock a championship lacrosse match would take place on the property between Kingsville and Harrow teams. For now the grounds were impeccable; by tomorrow evening there would be the aftermath where all workers would no doubt have an extra role to play in the clean-up. At the end of the holiday, though, the Mettawas would have conducted itself with style.

In anticipation of the following day's busy schedule, Betsy decided to check the few pieces that were laid over her chair, drying in her room. There was the bonnet that Miss Anderson had soiled when it blew off during croquet a few days ago. Betsy had been able to remove the grass stain with a gentle rub of salt. There was a pair of white gloves as well that needed to be returned to their owner before the next day's festivities. Of course, Mrs. Rankin had given her a silk kimono from Hong Kong to wash by hand. She said it would be far too delicate for the machines at the laundry. With a prolonged sigh, Betsy removed the robe from its tissue. As usual, she carefully examined the delicate fabric for any specific stains. She surmised that she would be able to spot clean the Mandarin collar with its smudged face powder, and there was what appeared to be a sticky smear of marmalade near one of the pockets. Betsy's face grew puzzled as she felt something weighted down in the fabric, something hard nestled deep inside. She slid her hand inside the pocket. Shocked, she pulled out two ruby earrings, glinting brilliantly in her hand.

Immediately Betsy went to see Miss Grimwood with the news and evidence, elated that she had probably saved Hattie's job. It was, indeed, good news all around. Mrs. Rankin, though relieved to see her treasured jewellery returned to her, found it not in her imperious disposition to apologize to the accused chambermaid. Instead, she admitted it was her own extraordinary caution and cleverness that had contributed to the situation. She now remembered she had hidden the earrings inside the pocket of the kimono for safekeeping, hung up the garment in the closet, and promptly forgot about them. No harm done, she had said. That was the extent of any apologetic overture to Hattie. Besides, Mr. and Mrs. Rankin were scheduled to leave the Mettawas in two days.

Miss Grimwood, though irascible and humourless most of the time, recognized a good worker when she saw one. She knew Hattie's efforts were exemplary, which was precisely why she had agreed with Mr. Wallace to convince the management to retain her. She also did not want anyone to say that her staff was untrustworthy.

Hattie's reprieve and subsequent relief could not have come at a better time, as she could enjoy the holiday along with everyone else, knowing that she could finish the season as one of the hotel's premier employees.

The Mettawas vibrated with excitement for days. Hiram Walker's favourite holiday had always been July 4th – his own birthday as well as his country's national holiday – and likewise, many of the American guests enjoyed not only the Dominion Day holiday, but also their own. Betsy understood this enthusiasm to celebrate one's country. Now that she had left England, she had found herself thinking about her country of birth in a different way; while she knew her new allegiance must be to Canada, she still felt homesick not only for family, but for the very land itself and the people's own holidays and customs.

When perusing a recent *Reporter,* she read with interest about the new society forming in the Dominion called 'The Daughters of the Empire'. She would have to ask her sister if a chapter had formed yet in Walkerville. If so, the two of them could join when Betsy returned to live with Emily after the summer. She said to herself that she would at least keep this Kingsville chapter in mind. The paper had encouraged every woman to be a member. There was even a children's society called 'Children of the Empire'. Articles such as this made Betsy feel somewhat nostalgic for England, and seeing the Union Jack and British Red Ensign assuaged her homesickness when she realized she was still in a part of the British Empire, though far away from her birthplace.

As the American guests were entertained by the Dominion Day's events, there was more to come when they celebrated their own national holiday. On July 4th there was a grand dance in the Casino. A few of the maids – Betsy included – stole away to watch the young couples flirt and dance. The Canadian Club flowed among the guests; even a few workers hid flasks in their pockets. Everyone enjoyed the brilliant fireworks which were set off safely on the beach at night, though poor Mr. Wallace and Terrence were run ragged as Betsy would later remember with a chuckle. Neither man was amused by the empty bottles of liquor found outside buried deep in the boxwoods!

The day after the party there was more than one request from a guest for a seltzer in the breakfast orange juice, or a dose of Hood's Sarsaparilla to 'rouse the liver'.

CHAPTER 14

≈

July, 1900 – Mettawas Resort, Kingsville

*I*T WAS THE end of the first week of July when Betsy received a call from her sister. Norman had finally arrived in Windsor the day before, earlier than expected. He would stay with Emily and Thomas, probably at least until Betsy was finished her duties mid-September. Then the two of them would have to decide their future path together.

In the meantime, Thomas could put him to good use in the glass shop. The furniture trend of cutting glass to fit the surface of tables to protect them from wear was making him very busy. The Globe Furniture Store in Walkerville, owned by the Walker family, had become a particularly good client. And an emerging construction industry in the Windsor area was creating a demand for windows for which glass of all shapes and sizes was needed.

Thomas would train Norman on the job, and would find the younger man anxious not only to start his life in Canada, but desirous of making enough money to begin providing for himself and Betsy.

Kitty looked forward to Norman's visit to Kingsville as well. She spoke to her friend of the entertainment they would have as two couples – she and Danny, Betsy and Norman. There would be ice cream socials to attend and picnics at Paradise Park. She had hoped that Danny would become the other young man's very good friend, just as the two girls had become practically inseparable during time free from their work. In fact, Danny had already offered his family's spare room over on Mill Street once Norman arrived.

The girls' plans took over much of their conversation, but inwardly, Betsy began to consider her own ambition, something she had not taken into account before the summer. Though she was glad that Norman was working with her brother-in-law, what about her own contribution to their union? Would she be returning to Windsor after the Mettawas closed its doors for the season? She had read about opportunities for women in the growing canning and tobacco industries. Norman would certainly hope to provide for the two of them once they had married, but in all truth, Betsy rather enjoyed the responsibility she had at the resort, and liked the positive comments about her work ethic. Despite Miss Grimwood's Rules of Decorum, she felt an independence that she had never really known before. She was quite certain that she would want to contribute financially to their household.

Other questions were plaguing her. What about the friends she had made here? They would be returning to their own families in the nearby towns. Would they see each other again, or was this the only summer when she and her new friends would find work at the Mettawas?

Betsy had been listening to a few of the other workers who had worked at the hotel since the place had opened, and who had witnessed many changes over time. On the surface the hotel seemed to be extremely busy, especially if one were to judge by the number of guests overbooked and arriving all the time. She had heard from Mr. Wallace that the Mettawas profits were not enough to sustain the resort. Despite the number of guests, the services and activities provided were straining the purse strings of the owners, and management was looking to cut corners. Something had to give, and Betsy hoped it would not be at the expense of the local workers.

These thoughts were preoccupying Betsy as she walked through the card room, the last of her rooms in the Casino to sweep through, tidy, and dust. She had already clipped dying foliage from the bouquet on the main pedestal table, and had refreshed the water in the vase, carefully wiping the water spilled on the walnut surface. *It really does need a nice piece of glass to protect the wood*, she thought, and smiled. It had also amused her to be leaving a pretty bouquet even in the bowling alley, but now when she thought about it, she wondered if it were really necessary. It seemed to her as though money could be saved by limiting some of those extra comforts. There had to be other areas where management could save as well; she would have to see what Mr. Wallace's opinion was in all this talk about dwindling funds. With that final thought, Betsy left the Casino, nodding at Terrence who merely grunted "hello" and waited for her to pass through the door before he entered the building.

The next day Betsy saw Mr. Wallace straightening a picture on the wall in the billiard room and approached him with her concerns. After listening politely to Betsy's suggestions, he tried not to reveal his amusement at the young girl's naïve comments. He knew she was trying to be helpful and he appreciated her thoughtful, well-meaning ways. She had exhibited a keen common sense, uncharacteristic of many young girls he had met there on staff over the past decade. He could not have been more proud of her if she had been his own daughter. It was not her place, however, to spend time on issues which continued to daunt even the treasurer.

"Miss Gooding," Mr. Wallace began after hearing her speak for several minutes so earnestly about business matters that really should not concern her, "you have no idea how much I appreciate your concerns. I see you have thought on this long and hard, and I do not mean to trivialize your suggestions. Not at all. You really do not have any idea, however, of what goes on behind the scenes – indeed, what has been going on here for at least the past five years, and even more so with Hiram's death last year. Yes, the Mettawas appears to have been a profitable undertaking and began as such, but in fact, management has been putting out more money than it has been bringing in to the hotel's coffers. It's as simple as that."

Betsy was about to speak, but he silenced her with his hand. "Really, I understand your concern – I really do – but I'm afraid that the fact of the matter is without the old man at the helm, the ship has been poised for a sinking."

He was about to continue down the hallway, but Betsy stood in his way with another question. She was perplexed by the man's cynicism.

"What about Mr. Walker's sons? I heard that they were very much involved with their father's undertakings, even when he was alive, but too ill to properly oversee things. Surely they will take every measure to bring more money to the Mettawas?"

With a deep sigh, Mr. Wallace continued when he saw that Betsy's queries would not be brushed easily aside. "That is precisely the point. Mr. Walker Sr. made no secret of the fact that he thought there was nary a sound business thought to be had among his sons, particularly pertaining to his dream of paradise here on the lake." Wallace seemed anxious to be leaving this topic behind.

"Well, if that were the case, why would Mr. Walker ever…"

Once again Wallace interrupted her, settling in for an honest explanation of the plight of the resort as he saw it. The young girl would not be deterred, he knew.

"I know I shall regret saying this, my dear, because I

do not condone the rumour mill. But this is a matter of public record. There was an article in the *Reporter* just last week about the appeal made by the Mettawas Resort Company to the Judge from the Court of Revision regarding the assessment of the Mettawas property which they thought was too high."

He paused to regard whether Betsy seemed to understand the implications of this. Whether she did or not, he continued.

"If the property assessment could be reduced, the hotel owners argued, they would have to pay fewer taxes. That obviously would help their financial situation. Would actually help the tourist trade itself, as a matter of fact. It doesn't seem as if anyone in council were truly listening, though. Or maybe they just didn't care."

"But why not?" Betsy persisted. "Surely they can see how important the resort is to the village? Look at all the tourists that come here every summer," she added, frowning in disbelief.

"That should seem obvious, I know," Mr. Wallace explained with a sigh. "The Walkers *have* argued in Kingsville council that the Mettawas brings tourists to the community, and that they would not come if the resort had to close owing to a lack of funds. Kingsville, they argued, could suffer in the long run from the loss of these tourists." By now, Wallace was checking the time on his pocket watch.

"I just don't understand why people who have been elected to oversee the well-being of a community can't be more reasonable," Betsy said. She felt herself beginning to lose patience with the situation and with this conversation.

Mr. Wallace sensed her discontent. "To tell you the truth, Miss Gooding, I'm really very worried that the resort's management will give up and offer to sell the place – lock, stock, and barrel."

Betsy's face blanched at the gentleman's passionate words which seemed to her quite desperate. Mr. Wallace regarded his pocket watch a second time.

"Really, I must be going; I have to meet someone. A pleasure to talk to you, as always," Mr. Wallace said as he quickly nodded in Betsy's direction, smiled slightly at her, and continued to walk down the hall.

Shaking her head at her friend's depressing comments, Betsy decided to think less of what might be in the hotel's future and more of what might be in her own. For her there would be new beginnings, not endings, because Norman was coming to visit, arriving at the Kingsville station next evening.

So much to do. A proper bath and hair washing tonight, for certain. She had already chosen what to wear: her new green skirt and floral blouse which she knew flattered her petite figure. Betsy felt a warm flush envelop her cheeks as she looked forward to what she hoped would be a memorable reunion.

CHAPTER 15

≈

July, 1900 – Mettawas Resort, Kingsville

M R. WALLACE HAD just thrown the tartan blanket over the smooth leather seat of the carriage waiting outside the servants' residence, now largely occupied by additional summer guests. He would accompany Betsy to the station and be a chaperone for the young couple returning to the Mettawas. He could see how flushed with nervous excitement the young woman was as she approached him waving and smiling broadly. On her head was a fashionable hat with green ribbon to match her outfit. With his help, Betsy stepped up into the buggy.

It would not take long to ride the three blocks north toward the Kingsville station. Along the way, Betsy could smell the leather of the seat and the horse's reins mixed in with the slight fish smell coming off the dock – a smell to which she had become accustomed. What she was not used to, however, was this knocking feeling under her ribs. The Mettawas Special would be arriving just before 6:30. It was now 6:15. *Could my heart pump any more loudly?* she thought.

They turned into the busy station, and after Mr. Wallace had tied up his horse-and-buggy, he walked inside the building to confirm the time. Betsy remained in her seat and waited. Finally, the train's whistle announced its arrival. She watched people disembark, and empathized with the uncertainty one feels when taking that first step down from a train in unfamiliar territory. Suddenly, all commotion ceased for Betsy, for there, standing on the platform before her, was the young man – the love of her life – whom she had tearfully left months ago in Ambleside.

Betsy was not surprised to see that Norman was dressed in apparel he wore for a special occasion: dark grey dress suit, tie, and Bowler hat. She smiled to see him turn to look around seemingly ill at ease in this foreign environment. She noticed he was holding rather awkwardly a large package which he now placed on the ground beside his small canvas satchel. His hands rested on his hips as he looked around for a welcoming face. Soundlessly, Betsy moved toward him. Though trying to appear reserved and calm, Norman, with a loud "whoop!" caught her in his gaze, and in seconds, engulfed her willingly in his arms and spun her around and around. Betsy laughingly tried to hold down her hat with one hand, all the while encircling his broad shoulders with the other for balance.

Mr. Wallace was at that moment emerging from the station and caught sight of the two locked in an embrace. Ever the discreet gentleman, he allowed them a few minutes for a proper welcome. There were tearful hugs and tentative kisses. Mindful of the other people around them, the two suddenly broke apart and regarded each other closely, looking for any change in appearance, and finding little, seemed gratified. Norman reached into his satchel and found the small tin of lemon raisin cookies Emily had baked especially for her sister. Shortly afterward, Mr. Wallace approached them, first eyeing the package on the ground, and then extending his hand.

"Excuse me, young man. Not meaning to intrude, but I have come to the station with Miss Gooding, and I'd like to help you with your things. My name is Maxwell Wallace."

"Yes, do pardon me, sir. I'm Norman Parker. It's a pleasure to meet you!" He extended his own hand which Mr. Wallace shook enthusiastically.

"Well, this is especially fortunate, then," he continued, "because I have something here from Thomas Gooding that I was supposed to deliver to a Mr. Wallace at the Mettawas. The package contains two pictures which have now been repaired, new glass replacing the old cracked ones." Mr. Wallace had already picked up the package that was wrapped in brown paper and secured with twine, and handed the satchel to Norman.

"Yes, well, I hadn't realized that you would be Thomas's delivery man. Thank you."

Mr. Wallace walked to the carriage, carefully placing the

package under his legs as he sat behind the horse and took up the reins. "Come on up, then. We should be getting back to the hotel."

The three sat on the seat closely together, Betsy in the middle, with Norman's satchel resting on his lap, his arm around his girl. Betsy was holding the tin of cookies on her lap and grinning from ear to ear, barely able to contain in her heart all the emotion she was feeling. Wallace, lips drawn tightly together, solemnly directed the horse back home, his thoughts elsewhere.

The next couple of hours were a whirlwind of becoming reacquainted. Betsy had so much to show Norman at the hotel which had been her temporary home now for four weeks. She knew he would at least meet Kitty and Danny before dark, because Norman would accompany the young chap to his family's home on Mill Street, where he would stay the weekend before returning to Walkerville on Sunday. Danny would be riding his bicycle so Betsy had been able to get permission for Norman to borrow one of the hotel's bicycles just for the night.

Betsy had wondered whether there might be an odd job or two that Norman could do at the Mettawas, but she considered that since the tourist season was already in full swing, there would likely be nothing for him there at the resort — that is, if he had even wanted to work there. In the meantime his job with her brother-in-law in Walkerville was a profitable one. She hoped it would provide him with a little extra for a ticket to visit her in Kingsville on the occasional weekend, at least until the Mettawas closed for the season.

They had about an hour left together until Norman would hop on the bicycle, satchel over his back, to find his bed at Danny's for the evening. Until then they would make the most of a walk together, which was about as private as their time together could possibly be there out in the open. Betsy waved at the guests who noticed them with some curiosity, patrons walking on the front lawn amid the lovely shade trees, or sitting on wooden benches trying to cool down in the refreshing air before the sun set and the voracious mosquitoes descended. Norman had already taken off his suit jacket and loosened his tie a little, feeling somewhat warm from either the company or the unfamiliar atmosphere, or both.

Arm in arm the two strolled along Park Street toward the lighthouse at the top of the hill. This longer approach to the harbour would allow them some additional private time to talk. Norman did his fair share of listening, though he was glad to hear Betsy's enthusiastic chatter about the Mettawas and its beautiful grounds.

She had outlined in detail her various responsibilities at the resort and described the Casino rooms, greenhouse, and even the 'Bridge of Sighs'. She had regaled him with stories of her relationships with her employers – with the close-mouthed Miss Grimwood and the garrulous Mr. Wallace. She had described the beauty of the sun setting and the glory of a full moon rising over the lake. She had even laughed when describing her first encounter with the most hideously huge, winged insects the locals called 'Junebugs' that had swarmed the streetlights the first week she had been here. She had talked about going to church with her best friend, Kitty, about picnics at Paradise Grove and dances in the Casino that she and the other workers could only observe, and the couples she had seen together on the gazebo when they thought no one had been looking. Betsy had blushed a little, but found she couldn't speak to him yet of how much she eagerly anticipated being part of a couple, too, like her friends. Now her fiancé was a real presence, not a stranger miles away.

Norman had listened intently, chuckling at all the appropriate times and showing an honest interest in both her business and leisure there. He had expressed surprise again at Mr. Wallace who had greeted him at the station. How exactly had Betsy met him again?

"My goodness, Norman, you're not jealous of him, are you?" Betsy had regarded her beau's profile. A shock of his dark hair tumbled over his brow. He had remained expressionless, but smiled at her when she had tightened her hold on his forearm. "You know, he's old enough to be my father! But to tell you the truth, he spoke to me first on the train the night I arrived, and I haven't had many older people here show any real interest in me or my background. He takes the time to have a conversation with me when I bump into him, which, now that I think of it, is usually at least once a day. He's kind of an overseer of matters here at the resort, so his job is to have an interest in just about everything here. He talks to everyone."

By now they had rounded the lighthouse, and had walked down the hill leading to the dock with its beautiful view of the lake. They continued to walk now in silence as they absorbed all the sights and sounds. The hotel had receded from their view behind them as their boots – having left the sloping gravel path – now tripped noisily along the wooden pier. The small waiting station where the steamers docked was in front of them with a few people inside and a few more milling about. There were four small warehouses to their left, and at a little distance to their right at the base of the hill below the Mettawas they could see the water-pumping station, the roof of which Betsy could see from her bedroom window.

Also to their right, below the Grovedale House, they could see several of Mr. Elliott's rental rowboats going out into the calm of the harbour, the people inside them laughing and enjoying their evening exercise. The day's haul of fish had already been taken off the tugs; one was moored and bobbing gently along the pier, the lake slapping against the wood of dock and boat. There was also the steamer *Imperial* which no doubt had brought in for the weekend several new guests to the hotel across Lake Erie from Sandusky and Cleveland. The harbour seemed busy, yet not busy at the same time.

After several minutes, Norman broke the quiet between them and resumed their conversation from earlier during their walk.

"Actually, I was more startled by the fact Mr. Wallace was the man I was supposed to seek first at the hotel because I had the parcel for which he had been waiting some time. Thomas had told me to be careful with it because it contained two watercolour paintings fronted by glass which he had cut especially to size since the original glass had broken. I think he said that they had apparently fallen off the wall and had cracked during some big entertainment here, maybe around the American holiday, though I can't remember now. I was glad to finally hand it over; I had been holding the package across my lap the whole time since leaving the Walkerville station!"

"Now that you mention it, I do remember seeing Mr. Wallace and Thomas speaking together at the station the day I left to come here, so I guess it makes sense that they would do business together. As it turned out, he ended up sitting with me on the train. I had no idea they had been business acquaintances before that meeting," Betsy said.

They had now reached the far end of the dock. Before turning around to retrace their steps, they stood for a moment, Norman with his arm around Betsy's waist, her head resting on his shoulder. The seagulls above and around them were shrieking, landing on the wooden dock or pecking at debris among the stones arranged alongside it, forming additional protection from the water. The birds' treasure could be a piece of crust dropped from a fisherman's lunch or a fish scale shimmering by the dock's edge like a lost jewel. Other gulls swooped down to closely eye the flotsam on the water's surface or to ravage a clump of moss caught between a moored vessel and the dock.

Norman spoke first. "What a beautiful night it is, lass. I've been dreaming of this moment when we could be together again. It seemed the day would never come, but now that it's here, I don't want to let you go."

Betsy enjoyed the slight pressure of Norman's arm around her waist, almost gasping aloud at the sheer pleasure of warmth she could feel through her whole body. She, too, wished the night would never end. Before she could say anything in response, though, Norman continued. "You know, I arrived in Halifax and took the train all the way down to Walkerville. I have had so much time to think about me...our future. Much of what I have seen in Canada so far has involved trains and carriage rides. There have been great expanses of land, but also the bustle of a city such as Toronto. Nothing like back home in London, of course, but you know me – I'm most comfortable on the farm where I grew up. So when I arrived at your sister's, I felt quite travelled out, and I haven't really experienced or seen much of this huge country yet." Norman paused for a moment and seemed mesmerized by the actions and calls of the sea birds.

Both gazed out toward the horizon where they could watch with interest the various fishing schooners coming into harbour for the evening. Somehow it seemed so natural for them to be standing on the dock together. They felt an affinity for this beautiful, grey, expansive lake which seemed so familiar to them, even though they hadn't been raised here. Norman already was feeling a connection to this body of water, and like Betsy, loved the rural atmosphere of this little village. Lake Erie was casting her spell and drawing him into an appreciation of her beauty.

Suddenly he turned toward her, his voice quiet. "Here's what I guess I'm trying to say, Betsy. As much as I'm so grateful to Emily and Thomas for all that they have done for me, I realize that I'm not fit for town or city life. I'm afraid to tell him that I don't want to learn the glass business. I don't think it's the precision of measuring and cutting hour after hour. I tend to like that part, actually. And I'm not afraid of heavy lifting. It's the confinement of being in that little box of a shop all day."

Betsy stood apart from him for a minute, and then took his hands in hers. She was almost afraid to pose the question, but she whispered, "What are you telling me, Norm — that you don't want to stay in this area? That you don't want to stay with … me?"

"No, of course not," he replied, turning back to gaze at the lake while still holding firm to one of her hands. "I love you Betsy. Always will. But I don't like the way my life here has started. I haven't painted a true picture for the folks back home, either. I've sent a telegram to say that everything is perfect, that I have a wonderful job, that the future is here. But something doesn't sit right with me. Am I wrong to hope not just to make money, but to work at something I really like, somewhere I love? You know I already have the person I want to spend my life with." At this point he looked at Betsy, who was relieved, he could see, but gearing up for a speech.

"Goodness, Norman!" she gently chided. "Who immediately finds what he wants? All you have ever known is the farm back home. You've helped your father, just as his father did before him. You've bought, cared for, sold, sheared, even slaughtered sheep! You can also make a wonderful mutton stew," she said with a laugh. "Don't be so impatient. And don't worry what Thomas will say if you no longer want to work in his shop. He's just trying to help us get started."

By now the sun was setting, half a blazing orb lying squashed on the western horizon. As Betsy and Norman turned to retrace their steps and walk up the hill leading to the Mettawas, they marvelled at the sky dressed in vivid shades of orange, casting a brilliant hue on everything.

"See?" Norman said lightly. "Who needs money when the world here is richly golden?" He kissed a wisp of hair curling at her temple, and they walked once again arm in arm.

By now Danny had arrived having completed his own work for the night at the railway station. He and Kitty were talking and gesturing at the row of bicycles locked away for safekeeping over by the Casino. After all the introductions were made and some easy banter ensued, the four agreed to meet the following day after supper, since the two young women would not be available until their day's work had been done. Danny laughed when he saw Betsy's wistful look and assured her that Norman would be in good company and that he would have the benefit of exploring Kingsville the next afternoon on his own, an adventure in itself, he had said, poking his elbow into his new friend's ribs. They needed to be on their way, he added with some reluctance, before darkness had completely settled in.

Before long the two hopped on their bicycles – Norman's on loan from the premises – and were riding in tandem down Division Road.

Betsy and Kitty returned through the 'Bridge of Sighs' to retire to their rooms for the night. Just before continuing down the hall, Kitty turned and said, "Peter wants Margaret to choose a few more of the kitchen and wait staff to pick wild blueberries down along by Cedar Creek tomorrow, Betsy. The cooks want buckets full because this week they're making dozens of pies for the reception following the children's show next Saturday night. I'm helping organize the event for the children, which seems an impossible task sometimes," Kitty added with a laugh.

"Sounds like fun. Don't forget your sun bonnet!" She smiled at her friend, then turned into her room, her head and heart both full.

Before going to bed, Betsy took her usual position by the open window for a few moments to look down below and fill her lungs with any fresh air that might be filtered through the screen. She thought of the conversation with Norman and sighed audibly. As usual, there was Mr. Wallace walking in the grove where the trees were the thickest, descending the hill and disappearing down the sloping path leading to the dock, accompanied by Terrence and his dog.

Under Mr. Wallace's arm was what looked like the

brown parcel circled in twine that Norman had delivered to him that very evening. How odd, she thought. Why carry a framed picture down to the dock? Not knowing what had got into her, Betsy defied curfew and reason to leave the residence and follow them.

CHAPTER 16

≈

July, 1900 – Mettawas Resort, Kingsville

I<small>T WAS NOW</small> dark and the guests who had been enter-
taining themselves outdoors on the premises had long
ago retired inside for the evening. The damp breeze off
the lake caused Betsy to shiver; she pulled her shawl more
closely around her shoulders, and for the second time that
day, walked down the hill leading to the dock. Unlike a
few hours ago when she had stood down there with Norman, there was now no one else around. There was the
steamer docked still, and she could see a light inside it. At
the base of the hill, Betsy turned right and walked toward
the waterworks station.

She could just slightly hear the hum of the pump, unless
it was the anxious beating of her own heart echoing in her
ears, Betsy thought grimly. Over this beat were the un-
mistakable voices. Dusty, the dog was tied outside near the

front of the squat building, its door slightly ajar. From her position toward the back end, Betsy could not see beyond the entrance. With the equipment, she guessed that there would not be much room inside for people – perhaps only two. She knew the voices had to be those of Mr. Wallace and Terrence. What she heard both puzzled and perplexed her:

"The steamer leaves for Detroit tomorrow morning at 8:30. I'll be here much earlier than that – the captain knows I'm coming. I'll get the rest in a few weeks. Funny, the only thing the patrons are expert at is how to have a good time. They certainly don't know a Cézanne from a Degas! Breaks my heart to see how the place and all Hiram's beautiful things are underappreciated, and not just by the guests – by the village, too. I'll be damned if I'll let these pieces in particular get swept up in any sale of the place."

"You don't think it will ever come to that, do you, Max? I mean, selling off the property? Bet Mr. Walker would be rolling around in his grave right about now if he knew the financial situation, with no relief in sight. I can't help but think that – eh? What's that noise?"

Betsy had inched forward to catch a glimpse through one of the tiny windows at the front. She could just make out what seemed to be several packages, about the same size as the ones Norman had brought to Kingsville, all wrapped in heavy brown paper, leaning against the wall, tucked behind the pump. Suddenly she realized that the dog, Dusty, had caught her scent, familiar to him given the number of times she had talked to his master. He had turned toward her, wagging his tail. Not wanting to be discovered, she quickly retreated, hiding herself on the other side of the squat building just behind its brick chimney, and waited.

"What's up, Dusty old boy?" whispered Terrence as he opened the door fully and approached the dog, scratching him behind the ears. "Just need a few more minutes and we'll be off to finish our walk."

Betsy watched as each man took what looked like three packages leaning against the wall and walked toward the docked steamer. When they arrived at the vessel, a man came up from below deck to meet them. The three exchanged a few words as the man took the items from them and disappeared below. Mr. Wallace and Terrence would be returning to the waterworks building to collect the dog and lock up the pumping station. Now was Betsy's only opportunity to leave unnoticed and return to her room. *Hopefully Miss Grimwood is sound asleep and won't have seen me leave or return*, she thought.

Back safely in her room, Betsy had time to swallow the rising panic that had almost overtaken her. She felt the need to talk to someone about what she had seen and heard, but who? It was well after midnight. The times she had seen Mr. Wallace walking late at night down by the docks made sense now. It seemed that Mr. Wallace was involved with taking from the hotel items that he didn't want anyone else to have – but what exactly? She had heard Mr. Wallace say something about how the guests would never know the difference. Betsy felt sick inside. Mr. Wallace – a thief?

Since Betsy couldn't wait for the morning to come, she walked through the shared water closet and knocked on Hattie's closed door.

"Hattie – psst – are you awake? Hattie?" she hissed.

"Huh? Betsy, is that you?" mumbled Hattie, sitting up in bed and rubbing her eyes in disbelief. "What on earth are you doing up so late?"

Betsy approached her bedside. "Sorry, Hattie... are you awake?"

"Hmm... I am now, apparently! What's wrong?" Suddenly Hattie was wide awake, alarmed by her friend's odd presence in her room so late at night.

Betsy did not see Hattie socially outside the Mettawas, Hattie remaining within her own network of coloured friends. But Hattie had expressed over and over to her the gratitude she felt when Betsy had offered her emotional support over the crisis with the earrings. Now Betsy needed, if not her assistance, at least her ear. Betsy knew that of all the new friends she had made at the resort, Hattie was probably the most level-headed. She never indulged in idle gossip, especially having been the brunt of it. Where Kitty could always be relied on for adventure and fun, she seemed to enjoy gossip just a little too much. Hattie, though, could be counted on to keep a secret. For that's all that Betsy felt she had weighing on her right now, a terrible secret, and that's how it should stay until she had some time to make sense of it. Maybe Hattie could help.

It was over an hour later – now approaching 2 o'clock – before the two young women came to the conclusion they should do nothing. Surely Mr. Wallace had proven to be a good friend to both of them. He had thought of a way Hattie could stay at the resort until her innocence was proven regarding those earrings belonging to Mrs. Rankin. Hattie insisted that she would never want to do anything that would hurt him. Betsy, too, felt a loyalty to the man who had been nothing but forthright with her, even confiding in her about some of the problems the resort was currently facing.

"Aye, that's the rub," Betsy murmured. "What do you think – could he be taking art from the walls? I know the glass fronts of two pictures have been replaced recently because Norman brought them here from the shop in Walkerville. Pretty clever, I have to say, to change pictures in broad daylight right under the noses of the management. Whoever would suspect that Mr. Wallace and Terrence – an overseer and night watchman – could ever have anything but the best interest of the resort in mind?"

"That's another point, don't you see? Maybe they *do* have the best interest of the hotel in mind. After all, they both have worked here since its opening. We don't know what Mr. Wallace plans to do with these pictures, if that's what they are. Maybe he's collecting some art pieces just for safekeeping, or moving them into another one of Mr. Walker's buildings. He does have several others, you know," said Hattie.

Realizing the mystery would not be solved that night, each turned into her own bed, though sleep did not come easily.

Morning came early for Betsy and Hattie; both rubbed their bleary eyes more than once the next day. Hattie joined the other chambermaids making the rounds of the rooms when the guests were at breakfast. Once when she was carrying some dirty linen downstairs to the area where Mr. Malott collected the laundry, she caught Betsy's eye, waved, and shrugged her shoulders as if to say, "Oh well, what can one really do?"

Betsy was lost in thought as she tuned out the banter of Mrs. Fox and the others. She had seen Kitty and several others of the kitchen and wait staff set off in a carriage with empty buckets, heading a few miles west to Cedar Creek to forage around for wild blueberries. They were wearing their sun bonnets, thankfully. Not something she would look forward to, she thought, with the sun beating down hot and steady on their heads all day. Her thoughts drifted to Norman. She was anxious to tell him about what she had seen last night.

Norman was having a busy day himself. He was learning about this village of Kingsville, and he liked what he saw and heard. Danny's parents had been hospitable and had even said he would be welcome in their home anytime. They assured him that there was work to be had in the village; the local sawmills were doing well with all the demand for new buildings, and real estate was plentiful, if one had the finances, of course.

Earlier that morning, before Danny had left early on his bicycle for his work at the train station, he had told Norman that he liked his responsibilities well enough, but the thought of working outside appealed to him more. He volunteered to be a fireman, he had said, because he enjoyed excitement and relished adventures that could even be dangerous. He had told Norman about the drills at the Mettawas hotel when he had first met Kitty. Recently he had heard how Mr. Conklin was looking to build a two-storey brick building at the corner of Main and Division, possibly as early as next year, and he thought he might try his hand at construction. Perhaps Norman could apply for that kind of work in Kingsville, too, Danny had offered. Norman had admitted he liked the outdoors, too. He was handy with a hammer and accustomed to lifting bales of hay, so he was unafraid of hard labour.

Everywhere Norman went there seemed to be evidence of a growing community. Every building around him, from banks to hotels to dry goods stores, had ladies and gentlemen entering and exiting with purpose. Well-dressed people bustled around him, always still finding the time to nod at an acquaintance or have a kind word with a passing friend.

It was now close to noon. Behind him was the Pastorius Hotel. He would check the menu posted on the front window to see if anything appealed to him. Perhaps a pint and some fish and chips for dinner would fit the bill. The

Exchange Hotel across the road and down a block might also offer a tasty alternative within his rather meagre budget. He decided to continue on and examine Main Street more closely.

Walking out of the Exchange an hour or so later, Norman hitched up his trousers and regarded the watch fob in his waistcoat pocket, a gift from his parents when he had left home. Across the street he could see that there was a barber shop; perhaps he should have a trim and shave and surprise Betsy when he saw her that evening. Before he could cross the street, though, he looked into the window at Salmoni's Dry Goods and caught the eye of a clerk who waved at him. Norman waved back. Then, almost next door was a sign in the window that caught his eye. The proprietor of Malott's Bros. Meat Market was in need of a meat cutter. 'Will train on the job', the sign read.

Norman walked inside and, avoiding the several fowl hanging from the ceiling, introduced himself to the man wearing a bloodied apron behind the counter who looked up and nodded at him, cleaver in hand. The barber would wait for another day.

By the time Betsy and Norman reunited later that evening, they both had much to tell each other, though his job offer would have to wait. Betsy's story about what had happened the previous night down at the harbour took priority. Norman was curious, though not alarmed; there was most likely a suitable explanation, though the words Betsy had overheard gave him pause. It was strange and out of character, she had added, that she had not seen Mr. Wallace all day.

Their stroll down toward the harbour was uneventful, however. The pumping station was closed, tight as a drum, and the steamer had departed. On the way back up toward the Mettawas, they encountered Kitty and Danny who were speaking to Mr. Elliott outside the Grovedale House, the small inn just east of the Mettawas. They were inquiring about the few rowboats that he rented down at the dock, deciding that sometime soon the four of them should rent one. Perhaps next weekend, if Norman could find the time to come out again from Walkerville. They all agreed that with summer soon coming to an end, they should get together and do something out of the ordinary; rowing a boat might be just the adventure for a memorable, romantic evening on the lake.

CHAPTER 17

≈

August, 1963 – Cedar Beach

*B*ETH CONTINUED TO be delighted by the fun Lake Erie offered. On especially calm days she would wade out to sit on a large rock that jutted from the water. When she jabbed a small British Ensign into one of the boulder's crevices, the rock would transform itself in her mind into a seaworthy vessel. Or she could float on an inner tube, anchored with a rope and pail filled with heavy stones. The raft she built with her father's help could on rough days be tethered to the wooden dock so that she could bob around on it, yet be safe from undercurrents beyond the sand bar. That the lake could suddenly change and transform itself was a lesson learned early. James had insisted his daughters respect the vicissitudes of Lake Erie, which could one moment appear peaceful and calm, but in the next become choppy with fickle winds whipping up foaming, cresting whitecaps.

It was a day such as this, a quiet Friday afternoon in late August during Aunt Betsy's second visit when the lake did, indeed, wreak havoc in the lives of the Dobson family, a day from which old Aunt Betsy would not recover.

Mary had just prepared tea which she took out to the front porch overlooking the water. On the tray with the tea things she always included a bud vase with a flower from the garden, as Aunt Betsy appreciated that little extra effort, and would comment if the vase were not there. This was the ritual before her mid-afternoon nap. Though she tried to keep her company, Mary bustled around Aunt Betsy, intent on dusting a shelf, or sweeping sand from the floor.

Perhaps it was because she would be leaving the cottage for Windsor in two days that on this occasion Aunt Betsy would have preferred that someone sit with her and chat. When Beth walked in the front door from the beach, comic book in hand, Aunt Betsy looked at her as if seeing her for the first time. She asked Beth to sit with her. Did she care for some tea? Perhaps a little juice? What about a slice of jelly doughnut? Now, there was the offer Beth couldn't refuse. She loved the treats that her mother bought every few days at the Kingsville Bakery.

"How are you feeling today, Aunt Betsy?" Beth asked, well-coached by her parents in the fine art of social etiquette with elders. She sat down only a little reluctantly beside the old woman. She had things to do.

"Kind of you to ask, my dear. A little weak but plucky, as they say! It must be the fresh air coming off the lake that makes we want to doze a little, I guess. If I close my eyes, I can almost imagine living here still with your great Uncle Norman. We used to spend a part of every day sitting here on the porch, looking out over the horizon. You know, I have lived near the lake just about all my adult life. Lake Erie never ceases to make me feel rather small and sad, and yet I'm still drawn to it. I can't explain it, really. I could watch it every day and feel pulled into its grey depths."

That evening, Elaine had been given permission to walk down to Cedar Island to meet her friends. They would be having a motorboat ride, just off Cedar Island. She assured her parents that she would still be back home before dark, one requirement they insisted she obey. Elaine had worked as a counsellor a few miles down the road at the camp for underprivileged children for the first three weeks of August, and now that she had one more week of summer before school resumed, she wanted to spend as much time as possible with friends she would miss when everyone returned to the city in September.

Dinner was a little earlier than usual, and afterward, James and Beth took their nightly stroll with Zippy, Mary cleared the dishes from the table for a quick game of cards with Aunt Betsy, Jean got ready for the arrival of her date to take her to the Leamington Drive-in (which the young man had mistakenly called "the Passion Pits" in front of a disapproving James), and Elaine headed down the road to meet her friends on Cedar Island.

Sunset arrived with its usual swarm of mosquitoes,

forcing most outdoor activity to move indoors. As the sun was going down, the sky was shot through with streaks of dark blue. One could feel the breeze shift as well, subtle at first and then fluttering the few pieces of laundry on the line until Mary unpegged them and brought them inside. Bullfrogs in the marsh, the chorus for the evening, sounded their low, staccato notes. The lake, once the placid playground for today's swim, was beginning to churn and reveal currents of water seemingly at war with each other.

The Dobsons looked at the mantel clock and felt uneasy. Though neither parent said anything yet, each knew the other was feeling a malaise in the pit of the stomach that always uniquely meant worry for a child. Dusk turned to dark, but still Elaine had not returned. Now everyone was uneasy. There was no way of contacting her. They would just have to wait, and pray that all would be well.

Darkness had descended, the tension in the air palpable. There was some discussion about calling Elaine's friends who lived on Cedar Island. Then their own phone rang. Mary visibly jumped at the sound. It was one of the other parents whose child was also missing.

"No, Elaine's not home yet…What's that? The boat hasn't returned yet? We had no idea…." James's voice trailed off as he motioned for Mary to grab the car keys suspended on a hook by the door. They would drive to join the other families already keeping vigil outside the teenagers' hangout, the small store on the Island. By now the waves were crashing onto the beach, the full moon over the lake highlighting the pitch and thrust of the water.

They contacted the Coast Guard. Police arrived. They waited some more.

Back at the Dobson cottage sat Beth and Aunt Betsy, both increasingly agitated by the turn of the day's events. The young girl stared at the frothing lake and heard the wind howling down through the chimney. She looked at the moon brilliantly illuminating the cresting waves, and thought of the poem her dad always quoted during such nights: "The moon was a ghostly galleon, tossed upon cloudy seas."

"Please, God, keep Elaine safe," Beth said half under her breath. She wondered if she should be doing something for Aunt Betsy, perhaps offer tea, or turn down the covers of the bed as her mother always did in the evening. She chose to do and say nothing but sit and pick up her book. Aunt Betsy had got herself ready for bed, though she was sitting on a chair, colourless and silent.

Before too long there was welcomed news. The Coast Guard had tracked the small boat, and had guided it back to the sanctuary of the Cedar Island dock. Thankfully, the four friends had been wearing life jackets on their joy ride; they had tried to make it to Put-in-Bay during daylight hours once they knew they couldn't make it home. Too much wind created an unmanageable chop in the water, and the small motor had been no match for the elements. Now, all four fell thankfully into the arms of parents who could not have been faulted for thinking the worst.

Once home, there was such a feeling of relief. Mary, unable to speak for the gratitude she felt having had her child returned safe and sound, turned to the stove to heat some milk and cocoa. Even James, who normally would take the opportunity to wax eloquent about the respect Lake Erie demanded and the insignificance of the small boat in her midst, chose instead to speak his mind to his daughter the following day. On this night he could say only what was in his heart, and he was just drained from worry.

"Auntie? Is it too late for you to join us for a spot of hot chocolate?" Mary called out, though Betsy had gone to lie down once she had heard the good news. Now, lying in her bed, the cover up to her chin, she looked frail and lost. Mary went to her side. "Auntie?"

Aunt Betsy's voice was just barely audible, and nothing seemed to make sense. Beth joined her parents at the side of the bed, observed the old lady mouthing words they could not understand. All they could make out from her incoherent rambling was something about a hat. She muttered repeatedly, "With only a hat...."

After Aunt Betsy's restless night, the Dobsons, now full of concern for her, decided it would be most prudent to return her to the Leaver Home where she could be attended by a registered nurse. Something had shifted in the old woman the night of Elaine's near-tragic boat ride. Aunt Betsy did not seem the same, almost as if the cloak of dementia had descended to mask whatever sense she seemed to have had left, or the churning currents of emotion deep within her had drawn her under. Never recovering from this crisis, by mid-winter, she was gone.

CHAPTER 18

≈

June, 2000 – Kingsville

*I*STAND AND STRETCH, grab a blanket, fold it beneath
me, return to my position on the floor. The pictures
from the cottage remain strewn around me, and I'm not
sure yet what I'll do with them. I reach inside and find
the envelopes with the newspaper clippings. On careful
examination of the dates that have been meticulously written in pencil at the top of each, I notice that they are from
The Kingsville Reporter and *The Amherstburg Echo*. There are
half a dozen articles, dated through the years beginning in
1900 and ending in 1953.

What had moved Aunt Betsy and Uncle Norman to
clip these articles? Why keep them hidden, safely taped
to the desk drawer, I ask myself. Most are about the Mettawas Hotel, but here is one quite different from the rest.
I unfold the yellowed paper, start to read. Immediately I

know that something tragic happened there in the summer of 1900. Something so heart-wrenching that Aunt Betsy had kept the article all those years. The headline of *The Amherstburg Echo* catches my attention and I settle in to read the shocking details:

DROWNED IN LAKE ERIE
Three Mettawas Hotel Employees
Swamped in Friday Night's Storm

CHAPTER 19

~

August, 1900 – Mettawas Resort, Kingsville

A MONG THE HELP there was a growing unease based on what they had read recently in *The Kingsville Reporter*. For them it confirmed all the whisperings and dire predictions heard as undercurrents throughout the season regarding the hotel's future. The article had stated that at the recent council meeting, the Mettawas Resort Company had pleaded one final time for tax concessions so that the hotel – which brought much tourism to the village, after all – could have some financial relief. The appeal had been denied by Judge Horne, and before long James Harrington Walker, who had spoken on behalf of the Mettawas, announced that the owners had no choice but to sell the property.

This would give new meaning to the end-of-season dance in the ballroom. Given the Walkers' startling announcement, a *last* dance could be prophetic. For the Walker regime, at least, it would be a final time to dress in one's finest and enjoy the orchestra. One last time to capture the spirit of Paradise on the ballroom floor. One last time to hear the dying strains of the "Mettawas Waltzes".

It was only the middle of August, and yet there was the inescapable feeling that summer's end would come before they knew it. Where families and couples could walk and play outside in July right up until 10 o'clock at nights, they were now beginning to notice dusk creep in shortly after 9 o'clock. For some, outdoor sports of swimming and golfing gave way to indoor activities of bowling and card playing.

Another week passed. The recent muggy weather had culminated in a huge thunderstorm, but the weekend coming up, the last one in August, promised sun and a clear sky, though slightly cooler temperatures. Every family at the Mettawas was looking forward to another children's show planned for Saturday afternoon. The community was invited to attend for an admission, the profits going to the three area churches. The kitchen had been busy preparing special treats for the event, including baking dozens of blueberry pies.

Hattie and Betsy had been talking in secret about what they had uncovered regarding Mr. Wallace's activities. Hattie admitted that there had been times when she had felt something seemed unusual when she was cleaning the card room in the Casino, but she couldn't place what it was, and let it go. Now that she thought about it, perhaps it was the occasional picture that had seemed different at the end of a hallway. Betsy had agreed. She remembered seeing a few places where the wallpaper was just a wee bit darker around the perimeter of a painting, almost imperceptibly so. It was something to which she just had not paid any attention. Who would, after all? But they both knew the answer.

Anyone who paid attention to that sort of nuance was someone who loved artwork, an art aficionado who examined paintings closely. Or perhaps someone who was suspicious, as they now were, and looking for something. The guests came and went, some here for a few days, some for weeks at a time, so there was always the sense that this was, after all, only a temporary lodging, with an active social life. What a perfect way to pilfer, the girls had to agree, in broad daylight and out in the open, particularly when the offending parties were the very people hired to ensure that the grounds and property were safe and in good care. After considerable discussion over a few days, the two decided against their earlier resolution to remain quiet. Now they felt they should say something to someone, but to whom?

"Well, I certainly don't feel comfortable pointing an accusatory finger at any servant here, given what happened to me," said Hattie. "I still think that if you're correct, and Mr. Wallace really is exchanging more valuable works for lesser ones, that he may very well have a sound explanation for it."

"That's precisely why I need to talk to him about it," said Betsy, though as soon as the words left her mouth she realized how presumptuous it would seem for someone like her to approach a man who was not only her senior, but also more experienced in matters dealing with the Mettawas. She really was in no position to cast aspersions on anyone. Furthermore, hadn't she valued their friendship? Betsy felt guilt over her suspicions. Still, had she not any sense of responsibility to the management which, after all, had hired her these past months? A few more days went by. Betsy carried about her business, as did Hattie. They did not speak again of this confusing and upsetting situation.

The last weekend had, indeed, been a confusing one, and not just owing to Mr. Wallace's secretive enterprise. Norman's uncertainty about his future was cause for concern as well. He had been away from Walkerville for only a couple of days, and already Norman had his sights on Kingsville as a desirable place to live. Imagine – Danny had put all kinds of thoughts into his head about finding a job in construction of a new building to be erected downtown. He might even consider volunteering at the fire hall, for goodness' sake! Norman had returned from a full day of walking up and down Main Street and in that one day had met more merchants than Betsy had over the course of an entire summer! People who had plans to expand their businesses and who might be looking to employ someone.

She couldn't believe it when Norman had told her of his conversation with Mr. Malott in his meat shop. He was looking for an apprentice. She had to admit that it was exciting to see how interested Norman had been in the proposition, one he would not have thought about himself. The window sign had just drawn him into the store, he had confessed to her, and the owner seemed to have taken a liking to him. He would learn a trade, or maybe it was a craft – she couldn't remember the exact words – and still be allowed to leave the confines of the butcher shop; Mr. Malott had told him the job also required delivering the various prepared meat to his customers.

Nevertheless, she knew that when he returned to Walkerville, Norman would be anxious about Thomas' reaction. Would he think Norman was letting him down, after all he had taught him in the glass shop? Time was of the essence. Mr. Malott wanted to know whether he would like to apprentice in his meat shop by summer's end, which was next weekend. "Nothing ventured, nothing gained," Norman had said to her with a smile, knowing that Betsy would appreciate her own father's words in the matter.

Throughout the week, Mr. Wallace would pass Betsy in the hallway of the hotel or from a distance outside, and she would return his wave, too anxious and uncertain if she wanted to have a more private conversation with him. He was usually speaking to Miss Grimwood or Terrence or consulting with one of the workers outside on the grounds. Lately he seemed rarely alone. She had to wait for the perfect moment; she had many questions to ask him.

The next Friday evening, the last weekend in August, Norman was arriving again around 6:30. This time, since

Kingsville was more familiar to him and he knew the location of the Mettawas, he assured Betsy he didn't need an escort from the station to get there; he would arrive on his own. He was nervous about what he wanted to say to Betsy, and thought that he could draw some last-minute strength in the three blocks down Lansdowne he would walk before they would meet again and have a chance to talk. He knew that Danny's parents were expecting him later that night.

The air, too, seemed to be buzzing with expectation. Some predicted an early autumn when they heard the flapping and honking of the first Canadian Geese flying low in their V-formation over the lake. Though it was still rather warm during daytime, the past week had seen considerable rain, and the evenings were becoming more crisp. Dusk drew together its cloak of darkness a little earlier as well. Where a month ago the guest could play croquet on the lawn until almost 10 o'clock at night, now it seemed that the sun had descended, a red ball in the sky, by 8:30.

Betsy had just taken off her apron and removed the small cap covering her hair. She was lost in thought anticipating Norman's arrival. While walking and tidying her appearance, she almost collided with Kitty who was emerging from the kitchen holding a silver tray filled with baskets of fresh, warm dinner rolls.

"All set for tomorrow," she mouthed to Betsy. That meant that both had received permission from Miss Grimwood to leave the premises the next evening, provided that they had met their obligations for the day at the hotel. The old warden really wasn't the mean taskmaster that they had originally thought after all.

The two were excited about their plans. Along with Danny and Norman, they would rent one of Mr. Elliott's rowboats right after dinner. It would be a romantic adventure, a chance for all four to have some fun together. They had looked forward to it all week.

That evening after he had arrived from the train station, Norman found Betsy for a private stroll where they could talk. He told her that he would be informing Mr. Malott the very next day of his decision to be available immediately to work in the meat shop as his apprentice. Norman had thought about everything and laid out his plan in the hope that she would give him her blessing. He knew that Betsy was particularly worried that he would be moving to Kingsville at precisely the time she would be finishing her work at the Mettawas and returning to her sister's in Walkerville. He tried to have an answer for everything.

"I was reluctant to tell Thomas that I would be leaving the glass shop since he has been so patient with me, not to mention generous with both his time and money. The wages he has paid me this month will actually help me get started in my new job. At first Thomas seemed very quiet, but then he clapped me hard on the back and said he was glad of my decision, and would even be honoured to help me purchase the tools of my new trade – any special knives or cleavers, and such like. Emily gave her blessing, too, Betsy."

At this, Betsy's eyes glistened with pride in her young

man's ambition and sense of purpose, and she felt grateful toward her sister and her husband who had been nothing but accepting of both of them. She smiled at Norman, though she felt anxious about this new, unknown twist to their future. Norman had said he would stay with Danny's folks for a few days until he had his own proper lodging in Kingsville.

That Sunday, Thomas, Emily, and little Edward would be making a day trip out to Kingsville so that they could bring the rest of Norman's things. Everything was happening so quickly. Though the end of August traditionally brought summer to a close, when many tourists would leave the area and return to their regular lives, the Mettawas itself was officially still open until mid-September. Betsy had only two weeks left, then, in Kingsville. At least they would have that time together, she thought, before she would return to live with her sister and help with the new baby. Everything was happening too quickly, indeed, but not in the way Betsy had anticipated.

CHAPTER 20

≈

August, 1900 – Mettawas Resort, Kingsville

*T*HE NEXT DAY, Saturday, was full of sun, the air and lake both placid. The children's show had been well attended. Everyone had indulged the little ones, even when they weren't at their best, because the audience knew that the modest proceeds were returning to the church coffers, perhaps an expression of goodwill extended from hotel management to community. And who could turn down a slice of one of those delicious pies?

Kitty was among the few staff from the dining room carrying trays of blueberry-stained plates from the Casino across the expanse of lawn and garden over to the main kitchen. She had seen Danny briefly when he had quickly bicycled over from the train station to explain Norman's change of plans, as he himself had received word earlier in the afternoon. Norman had sent his apologies, but he would not be able to go rowing with them that evening. Apparently Mr. Malott had wanted to work with Norman in the shop that day after it closed at 6 o'clock and had invited Norman back to his place for supper to meet his wife. Since they lived above the shop, they also had a room for him to rent there. He felt he couldn't refuse.

It was left to Kitty to inform Betsy of this turn of events. She knew that to say Betsy would be disappointed was an understatement. She was disappointed herself because she and Danny had been looking forward to spending some time together with the other couple. Half grumbling in the kitchen about the situation with the two cooks, Margaret and Peter, Kitty asked, more as a joke than not, whether they might like to go out for some boating fun that evening. As it turned out, they both seized the invitation with excitement; they just had to finish a few things in the kitchen and they could both be ready to go boating with Danny and her. They would meet down at the dock, they said.

By the time all the chores were done and the mess in the Casino attended to, it was almost seven o'clock, a little later than had been planned. Finally, Danny, Kitty, Margaret, and Peter left the premises en route to Elliott's Rentals by the dock. They saw Betsy, somewhat at loose ends, and she joined the four of them for the walk down the sloping hill toward the docks below.

As the afternoon had worn on, one could feel the stirring of a slight current of air, where earlier there had been none. Though the lake was very calm, Mr. Elliott had told the four of them to be very cautious out there.

"There seems to be the right conditions for a wind change, ladies and gentlemen, and I wouldn't have you flailing about now, in one of my rowboats. Be sure not to go out further than the end of the breakwater out there," he said, gesturing with one arm while handing another oar to Danny.

"Don't worry, sir," Danny had said. "I know we're a little later than we had originally said we would be, but we'll just go for a good row. Flex our muscles for the ladies," he said with a wink, "and we'll be back no later than an hour."

Peter crawled across the boat, one oar in hand, and positioned himself in the bow; the ladies were helped next and sat in the middle, holding their skirts closely against their legs; and Danny was in the stern, pushing away from the dock with his oar.

Betsy waved from the shore, though she had dearly wished that she and Norman had been the other couple in the boat with her two friends. She had never done that before, and she would have liked to have tried her hand at rowing.

There were two other rowboats out in the harbour this evening, and Betsy squinted at them to see more clearly. She recognized a couple in one boat who were guests at the Mettawas. In the other were three people she had never seen before, but thought they might have arrived just last night for the weekend. Everyone was laughing and enjoying the evening immensely, it seemed.

With a sigh, Betsy turned away from the lake and faced the hotel. It was odd looking up toward the servants' quarters from this vantage point. She counted the number of windows up on the third floor until she could just glimpse through the trees the orange glow reflected from the western sky on the glass panes of her window, where she had often positioned herself in the wee hours of the morning when she could not sleep.

Now she regarded the pump house over to one side with interest. From her bedroom window she could see only the rooftop of the building, and its tall brick chimney. From this current vantage point she could clearly see its small door and three small windows at the front, all facing the lake. The other three sides of the building were windowless. She gazed back at the few people down by the water who were focussed on the boats that were starting to bob, their occupants vigorously plying the water with their oars.

There was no better time than now, Betsy thought, to go closer to the pump-house for a better look inside. Gazing unhurriedly around her, she decided to walk calmly toward the small building. Maybe she could chance a look through one window, though all that she could be certain about was the darkness within.

Betsy walked toward the small building and, standing on tiptoes, peered through one tiny window. As her eyes adjusted to the dark interior, she wondered if what she thought she saw was the result of an overactive imagination. She squinted some more. Just poking out from behind the huge pump that took up most of the space was some light-coloured material wedged against the wall. She stepped away and pretended interest in the boats on the lake, and then tried again. Again up on the very tip of her toes she went. Something white lined one wall and was almost wedged in behind the pump – a textile folded over something to protect or hide or both. Was it canvas? Was it covering a brown-wrapped shape, similar to what she had already seen?

There were new voices coming now from the direction of the rental boats. The couple she had recognized had just come ashore. As she walked towards them, she could tell that they were happy to be handing over the oars to the boat keeper.

"Now, that was an exertion, I can tell you," the man said. "It started out fine when the lake was nice and calm, but once the waves became choppy, I could feel myself fighting the current."

"Yeah, I'll be glad when the other two boats return as well. I knew that the wind had changed, but I had thought that there would have been more time before the water turned rough," Mr. Elliott responded, placing the oars aside and reaching for the rope to help moor the boat. He would later drag it ashore with the others and secure them in the shed on shore.

"Usually the harbour is no problem," he continued, "as long as you stay between the arms of those breakwaters. It's hankering to be a storm, what with this wind shift coming right out of the west. That's never a good sign," he added, rubbing his head while looking up at the sky in the direction of the sunset.

Then the second boat with its three occupants came ashore, and they, too, expressed how quickly the elements had changed. The wind was beginning to whip up suddenly which made it a veritable fight with the oar to row against an increasingly strong current. By now Betsy had joined the few standing at the dock. She was holding her shawl tightly against herself with one hand, while with the other she was repeatedly sweeping wild strands of hair from her face.

The hour that Danny had promised to return the boat had come and gone. She had forgotten the pump-house altogether. She could still see their little boat, though, and was glad to see that it was still well within the breakwater's end. Betsy ventured a long armed wave in their direction, and was heartened to see someone within the boat wave back.

Turning away from the lake, she decided to walk back up the hill to the hotel. There was nothing she could do here. The wind was making it almost unpleasant to be about, and it looked as if her friends were on their way back to the shore. The message she had received from Kitty and Norman had been unexpected. She was glad that he would be starting immediately his apprenticeship, though today's sudden change in plan had unsettled her.

Her thoughts roamed to the following day when she would be reunited with Emily and family coming from Walkerville to visit. Suddenly all was right with the world. She had missed Em, to be sure, and she realized that the trip out to Kingsville by horse-and-buggy would be a little worrisome for her and her husband. After all, she was expecting her little one this fall. The thought once again of the generosity of her family over the last several months warmed Betsy's heart.

"Say — Miss Gooding! An unexpected pleasure to see you walking about! Where is your young man on this lovely Saturday evening?" Mr. Wallace had suddenly emerged before her as she was now walking through the grove and was almost back to the servants' annex.

"Goodness! He's... fine, Mr. Wallace. Uh — you startled me! I had been down at the docks and was just returning...." Betsy felt her tongue thicken and she couldn't speak without embarrassment. Had she been that preoccupied with her thoughts that she hadn't even noticed his approach? They spoke for a few moments about inconsequential subjects — the success of the children's show that afternoon, the sudden change in the weather — until Betsy could muster her courage and ask the question that had been on her mind for a week now.

"I've been wondering, Mr. Wallace, about something I saw and heard down there," she began, turning and nodding toward the pumping station behind her. "It was last Saturday night and — "

Before she had formulated the question, she caught the eye of Miss Grimwood hurrying out of the servants' building, holding down her skirts stirring about in the wind, approaching the two of them with a surprisingly animated bearing. Mr. Wallace left Betsy's side and walked up to the distraught matron. The older woman gestured toward the lake, shaking her head. It was clear to Betsy that she had not been pleased to learn two of the help had left the building without her approval.

She scowled at Betsy, who by now had joined them with an explanation for the last-minute change. Norman, her fiancé, had been unable to visit this evening, she had said, so Margaret and Peter had volunteered to go instead. No reason to worry, she continued, the four of them planned to return before dusk. In fact, they probably were on their way back now, she added to lessen the woman's disgruntlement.

Below them on the dock was another story. A few people who were still down near the rentals noticed that the third boat seemed to be moving in the wrong direction — out toward the lake rather than staying within the harbour's sanctuary. Mr. Elliott grabbed a pair of marine glasses and could see that they were at the mercy of the waves which were now running high.

"My God!" he said incredulously. "Whatever are they doing? Either they have lost or broken the oars! They're not even trying to row!"

News of the rowboat which was receding from view travelled quickly. Before long, the government tug, *Dalton*, which had been already lying in harbour, launched itself to apprehend the boat. Only with the marine glasses could one even catch a glimpse of the wayward vessel, now pitching and heaving more than a mile from the shore. Dusk had already stolen upon them, with a moonless night to soon follow.

All of the help at the Mettawas had heard the disturbing and frightening news. How difficult to believe that four of their very own were in such trouble. Though Danny had not been hired at the hotel, most knew him either from seeing him at the fire drills, at the station, or by Kitty's side. Nothing to do but wait, though, or go about one's own business.

As the night wore on, there was no news of any kind. The tug had returned after several dark hours of scouring the area. Its rescue attempt had been unsuccessful, darkness impeding any progress.

The vigil continued through the night, but one by one the servants retired to their own sorrow-filled rooms. At first only a few of the guests who had been outside the hotel had heard of the impending disaster, but before long, there seemed to be a pall cast on the entire resort – servant and patron alike. The light-hearted afternoon in the auditorium had yielded to a worried, sleepless night for many. Betsy and Hattie held back until they could do so no longer. Tears spilled freely, though they tried to remain positive.

"Are there other islands or bays out there in the lake where they might possibly have drifted?" Betsy asked, not fully understanding the size of Erie. Hattie wasn't sure, she had said, but she tried to believe that maybe a miracle would happen. Before the two retired for the night, long after midnight, they said a prayer together: "Please God, please bring our dear friends back to us – please keep them safe until morning's light can find them and guide them home." Betsy was able to cry herself to restless sleep, though shock, fear, and worry pressed deeply on her heart. And guilt. She was supposed to have been in that rowboat. She and Norman.

By early next day the grim message from Pelee Island had been sent and received by the hotel management. The rowboat had been found just off their shore; all but one male had drowned. At first his identity was unknown, but it was soon discovered to be Danny. Condolences could now be sent, though it was clear that the families and friends of Kitty, Margaret, and Peter would be beyond consoling.

What would have been a joyous reunion of sisters and young sweethearts became a Sunday afternoon heavy with grief. Betsy clung tightly to her sister, Emily, but she could barely speak for the sadness she felt. What made it worse was that the bodies had not yet been found. The thought of her laughing, fun-loving, irreverent Kitty alone and lost below in the dark depths of the lake made her feel a nausea that threatened to overcome her. And when she and Norman embraced, he, too, could feel guilt seep into his own veins like poison, threatening to arrest his own quickly beating heart. How would they ever recover from this? What private hell had Danny endured?

More news of the tragedy filtered to them. At 3 o'clock in the morning, the American steam barge, *Cumberland*, had found itself just off Pelee Island. The night had turned calm and had been quiet for the last several hours. Suddenly a small cry that became a yell had split the dark silence, and the captain had commanded his crew to shine their lamps over the water. They spied a young man drifting in a small boat, trying his best to raise an arm in their direction. Quick to respond, the captain and his men had managed to pull the exhausted young man aboard and revive him with a drink of hot tea with whiskey and warm, dry clothes. Eventually they had made their landing at Ashtabula, Ohio. Once they had been able to learn the fellow's identity and had coaxed from him his story, they had been able to contact the authorities at the nearest Canadian harbour, which was Pelee Island.

Emily and her family had already prepared to stay one night at the hotel; the carriage ride from Windsor had been long and uncomfortable enough for an expectant young mother. Now they would stay to offer emotional support to Betsy who seemed even physically smaller from the loss, hunched over as she was when they first saw her. For the management at the Mettawas there was an additional loss summed up in the hard, cold reality of losing two cooks and a waitress. They did not have to worry, however, because the community once again offered its support. The two hotels on Main Street and the Grovedale House next door each sent an experienced person to help for the duration of the tourist season. For the next two weeks – the last of the season – the Mettawas guests could continue to receive the quality of meals and service that they had come to know and expect.

It was the next day when young Danny arrived home,

the mischievous glint in his eye extinguished by an experience almost too terrible to describe. He, too, was made smaller for the horrible loss of Kitty and her two friends. Now he sat at the kitchen table, head in hand, his voice barely audible as he attempted to dredge the depths of that night's memory. His parents sat beside him, his mother's arm around his shoulder, his father and Norman doing their best to keep their own emotions in check.

"The wind had picked up something fearful, and the waves started to slosh over the sides of the boat. Peter and I couldn't even row, what with the currents tossing us in the opposite direction to where we wanted to go. We kept trying, but it became impossible. None of us knew what to do; we seemed at the mercy of the lake and wind." Danny clutched a handful of his hair while his mother tightened her grip on his shoulder.

"Finally we just had to lay down the oars because they had become useless to us. The water kept filling around us and we had nothing to bail out the boat. All I had was my damn hat. I kept trying to bail out the boat using only my hat." He grew silent.

The three listeners could hardly imagine the fear that must have overcome them pitching about in the hostile current.

"We were shrieking and yelling at each other, not knowing what to do, really, until we all managed to get together in the middle of the boat. We were all sent over the side of the boat seven times. Seven! Funny how I remember the exact number, and each time I tried to catch the women and managed to get them back into the boat. By now we kept drifting into the lake which was getting rougher. A little while later – maybe about a half hour later – another huge wave struck us, and suddenly we were all floundering in the water again."

He stopped talking for several seconds, and the others were quiet, heads bowed, waiting for the narrative to continue. "I watched two sink from view, then the other..." Danny whispered.

"It's alright, Danny. You don't have to talk about this now," said his father as he stood up from the table, torn by conflicting emotions of dismay and relief.

"No – once I get this out, I'll not speak of it again!" He swallowed hard and continued. "I could see the boat still beside us, and it had turned itself right again. I don't know how I was able to, but I managed to haul myself up and fall into it. The water, I think, must have been growing calmer. I don't remember how long I drifted like this because I must have fallen asleep. I remember hearing something, and then seeing a big black hulk bearing down on me. I had just enough strength in me to yell, and before long, there were lights cast across the boat, and the captain yelled back. He lowered his yawl and pulled me aboard. They told me later that it was 3 o'clock in the morning when their vessel had come across me."

The following Sunday afternoon the congregations of the area churches joined together at the tabernacle at Paradise Grove for a community memorial service. In time they might come to accept that the three lost bodies never would be found.

CHAPTER 21

≈

July, 2000 – Kingsville

THE CLIPPING FROM *The Amherstburg Echo* lies in my lap. I can't believe what I have just read. The way the paper describes the tragedy, it seems that summer storm on the lake must have come up too quickly. "How frightening for those poor souls," I say aloud, with only the ghosts of the past to hear me. Three young people taken by the lake made hostile by a conspiring wind. Or was it human error? I can't help but wonder whether such an outcome could have been averted. Did they even wear life jackets in those days? The lone survivor would never have been the same, I think.

I remain seated on the floor, draw my legs up to the other side underneath me, and rest my hands on my knees. I consider what it must have been like for a young Aunt Betsy to have worked there at the Mettawas. I look down on the floor beside me and reach for the snapshot of the laughing girls. Aunt Betsy must have been there at the time of the drowning. Had she known those poor unfortunate souls?

I consider the last visit Aunt Betsy ever made to the cottage. She had become very ill that August. Let's see... was I ten? Eleven? I retrieve the memory of another night when the lake's fury might have claimed a loved one but hadn't. Elaine had been found safe, after all.

Suddenly, the end to that terrifying night when we had all been so worried about Elaine starts to become clear. "Only a hat" was what Aunt Betsy had repeated while lying in her bed, and we had thought the words mere nonsense. She must have been recalling Danny's words as he explained what had happened all those years ago.

I open the news clipping again and read the name, *Kitty Bethune*. She was one of the three who had drowned that night. I close my eyes, draw in a long breath, and exhale. That summer at our cottage Aunt Betsy had been reliving the horrible experience of losing someone close to her. What terror, what unspeakable fear she must have felt all over again when Elaine had seemed lost to us. I can't help but return to the photos and recognize the laughing couple, signed by someone named Hattie, and then the snapshot with the three girls together, arm in arm during their summer at the Mettawas.

B., K., and H. Betsy, Kitty, and Hattie.

CHAPTER 22

≈

September, 1900 – Mettawas Resort, Kingsville

THE SERVANTS AND management at the Mettawas put on a brave face for the last week of the tourist season. Several of the male servants would stay longer to winterize the place – all screens would be removed and storm windows added. Emily had asked her sister to return to stay with them for a while in Walkerville after the new baby arrived, and that suited Betsy just fine. A new life could not make her forget the one lost, but she knew she would be busy, and that was precisely what she needed.

Norman's apprenticeship had begun in earnest and he was now enjoying room and board with the Malotts. He had told Betsy that Mr. Malott had shown him areas that were about to grow – Cedar Beach, for example. He planned to work hard, save money. "Who knows," he had said to her. "Perhaps one day after we're married we can even build our own little place on the lake. It would be a dream come true!" Marriage and babies and new homes took over Betsy's thoughts.

Since the Malotts knew Betsy would be leaving the area very soon, they invited the couple to a special dinner. They had wanted to get to know the young woman who would soon wed their handsome and clever new apprentice. The flat above their store on Main Street seemed warm and comfortable, befitting the family which had been so accepting of Norman and his bride-to-be.

"That was a delicious beef and kidney pie, Mrs. Malott," Betsy said. She delicately touched the linen napkin to her lip. "May I help you clear the table?"

"I'll hear of no such thing, young lady, not while I have two able-bodied girls who can help me." A meaningful glance in the direction of her two daughters spoke loud and clear, and they immediately stood up to the task with only a small, barely audible grumble between them. "I've made what I hope will be a suitable dessert for this occasion – a Tipsy Laird Trifle, Delbert's favourite."

It would be a long walk back to the Mettawas, probably a mile, but they preferred it, they said. They would have to be taking their leave shortly.

"Nonsense!" said Mr. Malott. "I'll bring the horse-and-buggy around for you. Treat the lady like a lady!" he added with a wink in Norman's direction.

The evening was clear and crisp. Over the horizon could be seen and heard a raucous flock of geese on their way from the open lake to settle for the night in the marshy areas along Cedar Creek. Betsy drew her shawl around her and was glad of the warm gloves she was wearing. They rode back to the Mettawas in comfortable quiet. Betsy leaned into Norman who was holding onto the reins of the horse, and laid her head on his shoulder with a sigh.

"A penny for your thoughts, dear," Norman said quietly. He was also feeling rather pensive. So much had transpired for both of them lately, events that were life-altering. It seemed almost unconscionable to be planning their future together when they knew what Danny was going through, and all that had been suddenly taken from him.

"I'm so exhausted from feeling sad, Norman. So much has happened here lately, and in a mere three days, I'll be leaving you and Kingsville behind. Please – couldn't you just leave Mr. Malott's buggy in our livery stable for a little while and spend some time with me – alone?"

There were only a few people in the Casino this evening, but just enough numbers to make the place appropriately respectable for the two of them to sit, to watch, and to be watched. After a half hour, Betsy requested that they walk through the beautiful Grovedale Park near the servants' annex one last time. She wanted to enjoy the comforting dark sanctuary of the woods that she would miss once she returned to Walkerville. For a while they rested there on a bench, amid the trees, just gazing through the branches at the crescent moon hooked in the dark sky over the lake. And as the mesmerizing lake view had done so many times before, it again attracted the two sweethearts, compelling them to walk arm in arm, leading them down the slope onto the wooden dock.

They were alone it seemed. In addition to a moored fishing tug, they could see the steamer, *Imperial*, docked against the east pier. It had come in earlier this evening and would be returning to Detroit tomorrow morning with some of the hotel's departing guests. They would travel down Lake Erie to the Detroit River, back to the American side. Now down on the dock, Betsy leaned down to remove a clump of grassy mud adhering to the bottom of her shoe. Suddenly she turned to her right toward the water station from which she thought she had seen a soft glow of light through one of its tiny front windows.

She pulled Norman over to one side and whispered in the direction of the squat building, "Look there – doesn't it seem odd that there's a light on inside? Why don't we go have a closer look?"

Norman, only too aware of the little time left to spend together, avoided answering her question by trying to fold her into his arms. Still, he could deny Betsy nothing. Seeing her inclined to investigate this strange light despite his overtures, he sighed, and allowed himself to be pulled by the hand in the direction she wanted to go.

They approached the pump-house. Both noticed that the door on the south side was slightly ajar. Norman's initial reaction was not to intrude where they were uninvited. "Not sure we should be here, Betsy," he said. "Come on, we really should go back. I'll need to return Mr. Malott's buggy before he – "

"Shhhhh! This will only take a few seconds."

By now they had quietly approached the building.

They could not hear or see anything. Betsy moved closer to the open door until Norman stepped in front of her. He placed his hand gingerly against the edge of the partially opened door to allow himself a clearer view inside; a moment later he was flailing on the ground in excruciating pain before going unconscious. Betsy screamed. It had all happened so quickly. All she could hear at first was the door suddenly slamming in their face. Norman had fallen down and she could see by the sliver of moonlight that a patch of dark was glistening on the front of his white shirt under his left hand, now flopping on his stomach.

"Norman! Norman!" she screamed. "What's happened?"

Norman's eyes fluttered open, and the door of the water station was flung wide. Standing beside them was Mr. Wallace, staring down at the young man in shocked disbelief.

"Oh, this is my fault! I shouldn't have dragged you over here to have a better look!" cried Betsy. She was bent over Norman's prone figure, her hand on his shoulder. His eyes were wide and staring up at her as if he had no recollection of how he came to be lying on the ground.

By now, Wallace was also kneeling on the ground, having taken from his waistcoat pocket a small flask which he raised to Norman's lips. His colour was beginning to return. Without speaking, Norman regarded his left hand, now bloodied. The older fellow took his clean handkerchief to wrap the mangled stub which had been crushed by the slamming door.

"Here, Norman, try your best to apply pressure to the top of your finger to staunch the bleeding. Looks as if you'll be needing a trip to see Dr. Wigle in the village. Come on. I'll drive you."

By now, several bystanders had assembled on the dock despite the late hour, alerted by Betsy's scream. News would travel quickly through the close community about what had transpired. Wallace, Betsy and Norman wended their way up the hill to fetch the carriage.

Though the hour had been late, in his home office Dr. Wigle administered a mild oral sedative and stitched up the finger tip, now ending just about at the top knuckle. After applying a wad of gauze and then a tightly wound bandage for additional protection, he suggested Norman return to the Malotts' residence and try to get a good night's sleep. He should return in ten days to have the stitches removed.

"It's a good thing you're right-handed, young man! It's also fortunate I didn't have to administer chloroform. Why, only last month I had a poor patient die from an allergic reaction while I was performing surgery on his hand!" he added. This only caused Norman's already pale skin to blanch further.

Betsy, herself pale and quiet, sat with the physician's wife in the parlour. Mrs. Wigle had already put a call through to Mr. Malott who had been awaiting Norman's return with his horse-and-buggy; now, informed of the accident, he was relieved to learn Mr. Wallace could drive his apprentice safely home. After Mr. Wallace and Norman said their goodbyes, the good doctor woke up his son and told him to drive Miss Gooding back to the Mettawas.

Following this adrenalin-pumping adventure, Betsy felt a

kind of numb relief and expectation that Norman would be fine. That relief, along with her grief over the recent drowning and the late night hour, brought her to exhaustion. She returned to her room, unlaced her shoes, unfastened her corset, and neglecting her nightly ablutions, fell into bed.

CHAPTER 23

≈

September, 1900 – Mettawas Resort, Kingsville

*T*HE NEXT DAY was routine. Rooms to clean. Linen and towels to collect for pick-up by the Maple Leaf Laundry. Last blooms from the greenhouse to arrange in crystal vases. If she hadn't heard from Norman by supper time, Betsy had decided she would borrow a bicycle and ride over to Malotts' herself after work. She had all but forgotten the business in the pump-house, but by now the other workers had heard about the incident on the dock the night before, and some approached Betsy to say that they hoped her young man would be alright.

Miss Grimwood was one person who wanted a few more details.

"Whatever were you doing down on the dock at that late hour, Miss Gooding? You know that no good can come from slinking about under the cover of night!" she added, a frown knitting her brows.

Should Betsy speak of her concerns to the matron who, after all, was the senior employee responsible for the welfare of the servants under her watchful eye? She decided to deflect her answer with one of her own questions: "Have you seen Mr. Wallace? I haven't seen him all day."

Miss Grimwood's eyes narrowed as they did when she was trying to determine whether something was going on under her nose or not. She looked at Betsy and didn't speak for several seconds. Then she said simply, "He's gone."

"What? What do you mean, 'gone'?" Betsy asked. She felt as if she were about to cry. She needed to talk to him. The matron's sagging posture alarmed her further. Miss Grimwood always had borne herself with shoulders back, chin up, but today she seemed different. Now it was Betsy's turn to ascertain if something were, indeed, going on.

Pursed lips gave way to a long, profound sigh. Miss Grimwood said only that he was unavailable, but would be leaving that day for Detroit. She wouldn't say if he would go by train, by steamer, or by carriage. As for her original question about what the young girl had been doing last night by the waterworks station, Miss Grimwood had waited, but the girl had not answered. Despite the older woman's natural instinct to disapprove, she suddenly and uncharacteristically felt her eyes warming – just a little – to Betsy, so earnest and warm-hearted standing there before her. As she regarded the seriousness of the young girl, the matron felt her own mouth tug upwards in a guarded smile.

"Well, Miss... Betsy... I do hope your young man will be well. On your way, then." And Miss Grimwood turned to leave the girl – eyes wide, mouth gaping.

First, she could not believe that Miss Grimwood had seemed so civil, had not even scolded her for being where she should not have been the previous night; second, the fact that Mr. Wallace was gone for good was most alarming of all.

Early in the evening, Norman had cycled over to the Mettawas and caught Betsy after work just as she was about to have her supper.

"Need anything, love?" asked Mrs. Fox of him as she took dirty dishes from the servants' dining room to bring them into the kitchen to wash and saw the fellow standing there, holding his hat in his good hand.

"Nothing, thank you.... I'll just get myself a glass of water. Thanks Mrs. Fox."

Betsy observed the large bandage covering the index finger on Norman's left hand, making it appear much bigger than it was.

"Don't worry, Betsy," Norman said with a smile, "I didn't have to use it to pedal here, you know! I feel much better than last night." He approached her as closely as he dared. "You know we need to talk about what happened," he said more softly so the other workers would not notice the serious turn of their conversation.

"I really don't know – everything happened so fast," she answered, lowering her voice as well. "I remember that the door to the station was ajar which is unusual, that there was a light inside the building, and that Mr. Wallace was inside. He must have suspected someone outside looking in, so he slammed the door, not realizing that you were leaning into it. The next thing I remember is the door opened wide again, you fell to the ground, and Mr. Wallace took over the situation. That's it. I've been mulling it over and over, but I don't understand what he was doing there. And, again, I feel terrible about what happened. If I hadn't been so curious about matters which didn't really concern me, you would not have lost part of your finger. I'm sorry, Norman," Betsy added and put her hand on Norman's right hand, resting on the table. "Does it hurt much?"

"Actually, it just feels numb today, though I imagine it will feel worse before it feels better," he said with a smile to lessen Betsy's worry and guilt. "Don't worry. Besides which, Mr. Malott said that to keep my bandage clean I don't have to learn about cutting and dressing the meat just yet. It would be too awkward anyway, what with a cleaver in one hand and a hunk of bloody meat in the other."

Betsy grimaced at the picture he was painting for her and then smiled at him.

He continued, "The good news is that he needs me to drive around his buggy to see what the customers might like to buy for their supper. It's a cart that holds an ice chest for various cuts of meat. That way I get to know more about our customers' likes and dislikes. Good way to see the neighbourhood, too."

Betsy smiled at his use of the word, "our", as if Norman already felt a part of the Malott business.

"I just wanted to let you know that I'm fine, but I promised the Malotts I would return before dusk. Last night took its toll on them too, I guess. But I can drive you to the train station and help with all your things, day after tomorrow," Norman said.

Betsy returned alone to her room and started to review the end-of-season chores that would occupy her the next day. Before slipping into bed, she stood by her window and gazed out at the night, crisp and cool, and thought about all that summer at the Mettawas had brought her. And cost her. With a heavy sigh, she slid beneath the covers.

The next morning as she opened her door, Betsy almost tripped on a rather large paper-wrapped package and envelope that had been leaning against it. Retreating softly down the corridor was Miss Grimwood, who now turned to acknowledge Betsy and what she, apparently, had left for her there.

"Oh, good morning, Miss Gooding," the matron said. "Mr. Wallace asked me to give you this package. He asks that you read the letter first." She hesitated a moment as if to add something else, but only said, "I shall see you downstairs shortly."

Betsy returned to the privacy of her room and sat on the edge of the bed, the package beside her. She opened the envelope to find a long letter written in exquisite penmanship:

Dear Miss Gooding,

By the time you read this, I shall be on the Imperial on my way to Detroit. I write this with mixed feelings. I regret that we were not able to say goodbye in person, and shall miss our talks such as we enjoyed this summer. I believe I owe you an explanation for my recent behaviour, and to that end have asked our mutual friend, Miss Grimwood, to deliver this package and letter to you.

In some ways you and I are kindred spirits; we have both experienced a terrible loss. For you it came unexpectedly with the sudden passing of your dear friend, Miss Bethune. I can not pretend to know the extent of the emptiness you must feel. For me, the pain was of a different kind. It descended more gradually, but overcame me, nevertheless. It had to do with the slipping away of Hiram's dream.

Have you ever felt conflicting emotions at the same time? Confusing, isn't it? On the one hand I knew that what I was doing was wrong; on the other, I felt such affection and respect for Hiram that I felt the need to keep twelve of the watercolours and lithographs from his special collection, a collection that he and I had built over the last twenty years together. These were paintings acquired through auction and estate sales that he would ask me to attend with him. He would tell me that his own sons did not seem to express the same interest he had in art, and in me he saw a similar passion to his own. To be honest, some of these pieces have more sentimental value than monetary. I felt – and feel – a real loyalty to the man. In many ways he treated me as his son.

Hiram had arranged to have almost four hundred pieces of fine art to hang in what he believed could be a true spot of Heaven on

Lake Erie, here at the Mettawas. He told me that he wanted his guests to think of the hotel as their home, with the finest luxuries and comforts he could provide for them. When I saw the disrespect and carelessness that a few patrons showed when they (no doubt being full of drink) caused two paintings to fall off the wall, and then left both the broken glass and the paintings on the floor for one of us mere employees to find the next day, I knew that I had to act.

Actually, I had already been thinking about what I wanted to do. During my late night walkabouts with Terrence which you had observed, apparently, from your window, I had been watchful of opportunities down at the dock. It was during these sojourns when I made the acquaintance of the captain of the Imperial.

I enlisted the help of Terrence, whom you know to be as loyal and steadfast an employee as I am, though that might seem ironic to you once you have read this. Please believe me when I tell you that what I did was out of love for an old man and his dream. Since people were accustomed to seeing both Terrence and myself throughout the resort both day and night as guardians of the property, it was not difficult to move a few paintings around and remove a few altogether over a period of time. Two paintings one day, another two a few days later, and I soon had the twelve in my possession. Twelve of almost four hundred works of art! Who would miss them? Certainly not the hotel owners! Nor the guests, for that matter.

We wrapped each piece carefully for protection, and then covered them with additional canvas to keep out the damp. There was not much room in there, so we hid only a few at a time. On two separate occasions when the Imperial *docked in the harbour at night, I had arranged with the captain to store six packages of varying sizes so that they would already be on board when either Terrence or I would take the steamer back to Detroit for the day. As you know, on occasion Mettawas business would take me to Detroit and then I would return by train the same day.*

I had returned a couple of nights ago to the water pumping station to ensure that all was intact, that there was left behind no incriminating evidence. When I heard steps outside and suspected someone was about to enter, I slammed the door, apparently too vigorously. You must believe me when I tell you I was as shocked and pained to see you as you were to see me.

Now to the package. Yes, irony of ironies. It is a picture, one that I am most fond of, and one of the lithographs from my own small collection. You need not worry; it is fully paid for, though I suspect that you and especially Norman feel you have paid quite handsomely already.

Please accept this gift prior to your happy wedding day which I understand will arrive in the near future. I would like to think that the lovely lady in the picture accepting a cup of tea from the wee child might be you someday in your own happy home. You most certainly deserve such a bright future.

As for my own future, after the recent events have been exposed, I know that the Walker brothers will be forced to contend with me. I don't know what course of action they will take; after meeting with me yesterday, they are not certain themselves. One thing is for sure, though. I shall never again be returning to the Mettawas.

Most sincerely yours,

Maxwell Wallace

For several minutes Betsy sat in shocked silence, trying to process what she had just read. Very carefully she removed the wrapping from the picture. The image there was just as Mr. Wallace had described, and that, along with his sentiments, brought more than a few tears to her eyes. She was relieved on the one hand to learn something had been going on and it wasn't only her overactive imagination; on the other, though, she worried about what might be in store for her friend, given his covert activities. How wonderful that he had thought enough of their friendship to want to say goodbye, and even to give her a wedding gift.

"Conflicting emotions at one time, Mr. Wallace?" she asked out loud. "Indeed!"

Betsy set the picture and letter gently on the bed and left the room, still crying, yet with a smile on her face.

CHAPTER 24

≈

July, 2000 – Kingsville

*T*HESE YELLOWING BITS of paper have been a startling revelation. One article says that an American, Mr. Beyers, bought the original Mettawas resort from the Walkers in 1901, that he spent considerable money refurbishing the place, yet within two years, tore down most of the resort due to disagreements with the town council over tax assessments.

"Unbelievable," I mutter. I hear footsteps coming downstairs.

Graeme joins me, surprised to see me lost in thought and sitting on the floor amid papers and photos.

"Hey – I've been looking for you. What are you doing down here?" he asks.

"Says here, Graeme, that the new owner of the Mettawas Hotel actually destroyed most of it when he didn't get town council's approval for a reduction in taxes. Can you believe it?"

"Really? Well, why didn't the town give the resort a break? After all, it must have been a fantastic draw for tourists."

"Who knows?" I say. "I just find it all rather sad. Such a great looking resort it was, down at the lake. You'll have to look at these pictures. I've been reading some interesting articles about the place." I hand him a few of the newspaper clippings and he sits down on the floor beside me.

"Who knows now what the politics were at the time?" I show him a picture of what the Mettawas once looked like in the beginning, and then the other news article with the image of a much less imposing and somewhat unremarkable building.

"Looks like a much smaller building was built on part of the ruins – called the Mettawas Inn – in 1914. I remember my father telling us that he and his family had been at the grand opening. And you know what? That place was eventually called the Lakeshore Terrace Hotel, you know, that derelict building that burned down a few months ago? Who knew it had such a history?"

By now Graeme is reading the articles I have thrust into his hands.

I return to the snapshots on the floor beside me. One in particular grabs my attention yet again, the one with the three laughing girls, arms congenially around each other, posing for the camera in front of a building I know now to be the entrance to the old Mettawas Hotel. Betsy, Hattie, and Kitty.

Here's another picture of Hattie with her family taken several years later, apparently — she smiling with her husband and two children, all standing on the sandy beach outside Betsy and Norman's place. When I turn over the picture, the words *Hattie, Aaron, Robert, and Frank at Cedar Beach*. It's obvious the young women's friendship extended beyond their time working together in 1900. I see the cottage in the background, so I assume Aunt Betsy is standing at the water's edge taking the picture.

Another moment frozen in time: it's Aunt Betsy in this one, laughing, holding Hattie's child. I feel an unfamiliar regret. At the time had Aunt Betsy wanted to have children, too? After all, Uncle Norman had built a rather imposing home for his bride — one with three bedrooms, much grander than the other two he had built beside it.

Had life disappointed her? I look again at the picture and see the smile on her face. She looks so comfortable, so in her element at the lake. Had Aunt Betsy felt like a mere guest when she had been at our place for a week at a time? Why couldn't I have asked more questions, taken more of an interest in the words she spoke to me?

Finally, a picture of me with Aunt Betsy. This one shows us hanging a few clothes items on the line to dry. I am smiling at the old lady who bows slightly toward me, turning her head toward the camera, smiling subtly, even playfully. Judging from these photographs, Aunt Betsy must have had a remarkable summer at the Mettawas, all those years ago. She would have had quite a story to tell over the years, if our family had only been listening.

All of a sudden my reverie is broken by Graeme, who has been talking now for a few minutes. Nothing he has said has registered with me.

"Wouldn't you agree?" I hear him ask, and by the apparent blank expression on my face, he knows to repeat himself.

"As I was saying, Beth, now that the summer is half over, I'm glad to see you tackling what's left of the things from the cottage. You can finally get some closure."

I fully hear him this time, but my gaze cannot leave the photographs of the Mettawas, and of Betsy as a young woman alongside her two friends who clearly had meant so much to her. My finger traces the handwriting on the back of the framed lithograph, the wedding present Betsy had received. I am lured to another place and time; my husband's words, though well-intentioned, ring hollow.

ACKNOWLEDGEMENTS

This story grew from my interest in personal family history and in local history, particularly regarding Hiram Walker's influence on my town, Kingsville, and the tourist attraction he built on the lake in 1889 called the Mettawas Hotel.

I found the two volumes of *Kingsville 1790-2000: A Stroll Through Time* by the Kingsville-Gosfield Heritage Society most helpful. Special thanks to Marilyn Armstrong-Reynolds, archivist at the Kingsville Archives, who was happy to share with me any pertinent information from their files and also lead me in the right direction when I had a question. When reading excerpts from *The Amherstburg Echo* at the Archives I learned of the real drowning of three Mettawas workers in the fickle waters of Lake Erie. That tragedy was my inspiration for the episode that occurs in this story.

Thanks also to the office of *The Kingsville Reporter* where the old articles and advertisements could offer me a glimpse of life in Kingsville in 1900.

I also learned more about the early Kingsville community through www.divisionoftime.ca.

In terms of personal family history, a found passport of my own Great Aunt Betsy and Great Uncle Norman at the family cottage was the catalyst for creating and motivating my characters. I have no idea what my own Aunt Betsy's early life in Canada had been like; I decided to imagine her working for the summer of 1900 at the Mettawas in the resort village of Kingsville. Further, I loved considering how tourists travelled here by train or steamer to enjoy all the luxuries of the beautiful Mettawas Hotel. I can't help but wonder what the town would look like today if the resort still existed as Hiram Walker had envisioned it.

This is, however, a work of fiction. Creating a semblance of what life might have been like in 1900 is a far cry from offering only facts and truth. I hope that there is an air of authenticity around the different time frames and places. Any and all factual errors (or creative distortions of truth) are my doing alone.

The year 1963 is easier for me to call up since I have lived through that time period. With due respect to my own two sisters and their husbands, I hope that they will enjoy what I have taken (or embellished) from our own history and summers at the cottage at Cedar Beach.

Thank you to my brother-in-law, Ian Hundey, for his careful reading, comments, and suggestions.

I especially want to thank my daughters, Allison and Lauren, for their many hours of thoughtful editing and patient willingness to talk to me about the characters as if they were real. They have spent much time assisting me at the computer.

Thank you to Laurie Smith, editor at Cranberry Tree Press.

Lastly, a heartfelt thank you to my son, Andrew, for his quiet encouragement, and to my supportive husband, Ray, who may see a little of himself in these pages.

NOTES

The four-lined verse at the beginning of the novel is from a poem printed on a copper plate found buried on the former Mettawas Property to the west of the Lakeshore Terrace Hotel on April 17th, 2000, the day the hotel burned to the ground.

Due to the decorative scrollwork around the poem, it is believed that the plaque was likely mounted in the Mettawas Hotel or the Casino Building by the Walker family.

From *Kingsville 1790-2000: A Stroll Through Time,* Vol.1, p.126. Published by the Kingsville-Gosfield Heritage Society, 2003

CRANBERRY TREE PRESS

The text of this book is set in Bembo,
designed in 1929 by Stanley Morrison
for the Monotype Corporation.
It was modelled on typefaces
cut by Francesco Griffo in 1495.

The book was printed and bound by
Marquis Imprimeur, Inc. in Quebec, Canada.